In memory of my Mum, Deborah Reid.

The truest Warrior and kindest soul.

You were the sweetest Mother of all and your love of the written word is the inspiration behind everything I do.

You are carved into the soul of every word I write.
I love and miss you immeasurably.

Chapter One

The punch to my mouth didn't hurt as much as knowing I'd let my guard down.

James, my best friend since I was fourteen and colleague on the Greater Manchester Police force, stepped back five paces to allow me room to breathe, a look of complete smugness on his face.

We had been sparring in the gym for the past hour and we have never and will never hold back on each other. James doesn't care that I'm a woman. He doesn't care that we're friends. In the real world, a criminal wouldn't care either. People aren't always good.

He looked down at his bare fist, ("Who wears gloves outside the ring?"), at the blood smeared across his knuckles. My blood. He looked up at me as I touched the lip he'd just bust as I'd bit it upon impact. He held up his hands. "Sorry Loz."

He grunted between ragged breaths, wiping a droplet of sweat from his brow. 'Loz.' His nickname for me when we're not working. On duty, it's 'Constable Smith.' 'Smith.' What a boring, nonsensical, uninteresting last name. I'd always wanted a cool, MI5-worthy spy name. "Constable Steel is the name, Lauren Steel." Or just…Steel. No constable, no Lauren. Yeah. Steel.

"What're you, concuss?" James teased. I realised I was staring at the blood on the tip of my index finger, pondering my dull name. I didn't say a word, but simply round house kicked him in the side. His guard was down this time, and his tall, lean figure, toppled against the ropes and slid to the floor.

Not giving him a moment to recover, I used my favourite technique, learned after years of practice in Jiu Jitsu. I slid along the floor, wrapped my legs around his neck and pinned his hands at a twisted angle on the floor. After a moment of struggle, he'd tapped my legs twice. I released him from my hold, staggered up off the floor and leaned my hands on my knees for support as I laughed at his disgruntled behaviour. He pulled himself up, holding his throat.

"You good?" I taunted? "Finished?" He nodded by way of response and walked over, his fist outstretched in the sign of 'Truce.' I tapped it with mine and we climbed out of the ring.

We sat on a workout bench inside the cold, concrete gym. The gym was empty, due to the late hour. That's the life of a copper. You can't choose a career in law enforcement and expect a nine-till-five schedule. One week, you're on stakeouts from dark till light. The next, you're catching up on a mountain of paperwork from that one drunk driver you nicked for running over a child's bicycle. But I liked it that way. No two days were the same, something exciting always going on and I got to work with my best friend.

It was the life I'd always dreamt of… though I suppose I always knew something was off. Something not quite right about my place in the world. Never knowing where I came from, the baby girl with flaming red hair, left at the side of the road. In and out of foster care until I was fourteen. Hoping to fix my anger issues, a social worker with coffee breath and frizzy blonde hair enrolled me into a mixed martial arts class at the community centre. Sensei Clarke paired me up with his sixteen-year-old son, James, trusting him to lead this troubled teenage girl down the right path.

I took one look at that gorgeous olive-skinned face, golden-brown eyes and floppy brown hair… and kicked him straight between the legs. He fell to the floor, recovered from his agony in an impressive twenty seconds, and came back with a sweet kick to my stomach that sent me flying. He didn't care where I came from, or that I was a girl, or that I was 'troubled' (as per my notes). He towered over my winded body, held out his hand and said, "If you act like a brat, I'll treat you like a brat. If you respect me, I'll respect you." From that moment, I knew I loved him. I pounced off the floor, threw myself on top of him and pummelled him square in the nose. It took Sensei Clarke and five students to pull me off.

Within a year, James and I were inseparable. My social worker left and my new social worker – who smelt of Lavender and kept her hair in a tightly controlled ponytail - wanted to pull me out of the class, but by that time Sensei Clarke had fostered me and that was not going to happen.

By the time we were old enough to move out, James and I had both joined the Police as volunteers. I got my own flat, but I still saw James just as much as when we had lived together. We worked our shifts most of the day, beat each other up for a few hours, hung out for a few more and then slept the rest (in separate beds). I was still, of course, absolutely in love with him. How could I not be? He was *that* person in my life, who I knew, no matter what, would be there for me. He'd beaten up disrespectful men in bars for me, he'd taught me how to handle myself as a woman in a job dominated by men. James was everything to me but I couldn't tell him a word of it. I know how these things go. I'd tell him how I felt, I'd confess my deepest most heartfelt emotions and devotion for him and he, in turn, would absolutely not feel the same way.

He caught me looking at him. Awkward.

"You good?" His go-to when he doesn't really want an honest answer.

"Uh-huh. You?"

"Yup."

"Good."

"Good."

We laughed and bumped shoulders. "Shall we get off?" I asked, hoping he didn't fancy an hour's cardio on the treadmills. He nodded his head. Sweat flicked onto the floor.

"You in tomorrow, yeah?" he asked, swinging his gym bag onto his shoulder.

I nodded.

"Cool." He shoved me playfully and pointed to my lip. "Get some ice on that."

I gave him a thumbs up. "Will do." Prick.

He left the gym through the shutters that had been left up to allow air to run through the building. I considered staying for a little longer and lifting some weights. There was always this urge to push myself a little further, but to not share my progress with James, so that one day we'd be sparring in the ring and I'd pull out some amazing move he'd never practised before, or hit him with an incredible strength because I'd secretly been building muscle. I was always thinking of ways to impress him. He was the type who would check out the pretty blonde girl, or the cute brunette with the blue eyes, but he would only ever date the girls who he thought could kick his arse in the gym or teach him something new about the ways of the world. I dreaded the day he found a girl he enjoyed spending more time with than me. A smug part of myself couldn't actually see that being possible. Never say never.

I had started switching off the lights when I saw his white BMW pull out of the car park and around the corner towards the main road. The BMW, I was sure, had been purchased on finance to impress girls. I'd thought it transparent, but supposed some girls are into that kind of thing. A car is a car.

I pulled down the shutter and clipped the padlock into place, before hiding the key behind a brick in the wall for the owner, Tony Marquess, tomorrow morning. Marquess. Now there was a nice last name. Sounded French but I knew Tony had come from North Manchester...perhaps his family were French.

That was the chain of thought I'd had as I'd wandered over to my car, which was parked in the corner by a row of trees which led into an industrial estate.

The night sky was crystal clear. If it had been November, the road would have been covered with a thin sheet of frost and I would have had to run my car for a good twenty minutes to clear the ice from my window screen. I wished it had been November. The sparring had left me covered in a sheen of sweat and my t-shirt was sticking to my back and front. I was one big, frizz ball of heat exhaustion and the smoggy weather didn't help. Of course, if it had been November and freezing cold, I would have complained about that too. Typical Brit, never happy with the weather.

 I'd been imagining myself in a cold shower while searching the side pockets of my gym bag for my keys, when I noticed a mysterious figure leaning over me in my window. People had snuck up on me before. My intent was to send this joker to A&E with a broken nose, a broken arm and a bruised ego. Unfortunately for me, this wasn't some stupid kid or even some creep who thought he could take advantage of a lone woman in the dark. No. This person had been trained. As I swung my body round and threw my gym bag in their face, they deflected it with ease, glided towards me like the wind and plunged a dagger into my chest.

 I gasped in shock as the pain swelled and instantly faded. My body filled with adrenaline as my brain commanded me to fight back. But, how could I? There was a dagger in my chest and the person who wielded it was impossibly fast and strong. My hand grasped at the dagger in disbelief. It felt strange and bumpy. I tried to look down at it and saw some foreign language etched into the blade.

I looked up, the world starting to twist and blur before me. I blinked back tears.

The assailant, all in black stepped forward and put their gloved hands over mine where they held the hilt. I tried to look into their eyes but saw nothing. I tried to plead with my eyes as I felt something cold soak into my top and down my stomach. I was trying to say, "Please don't pull it out. If you leave it in, I might survive. If you pull it out, I'm dead in seconds."

They ignored my unspoken pleas. The mysterious figure pulled the dagger out of my chest and an ice-cold rush wriggled down my face, torso and legs. I hit the floor but it didn't hurt. Nothing hurt.

Okay, I thought, as I lost consciousness. *This is where I die.*

All I wanted when I woke up was to see the face of the person who had done this. I moaned as I managed to flip myself onto my back. Instead of my killer, however, I saw something beautiful.

The moon.

Okay, I thought. *This isn't so bad. I can't feel the pain anymore, which I guess is a bad sign. It's warm at least…though I'm getting cold somehow. I wish I'd had a chance to fight back. James would be disappointed. Would he? Would he forgive me? I suppose there are worse ways to die. I was lay on…what? Concrete? Wet concrete? Oh. It hasn't rained for weeks. I'm lay in my own blood. That's a lot of blood.* Not for the first time, I asked myself, *How am I still alive?*

I managed to lift my hand towards my head. My hand swayed and collapsed to the side of me. My fingers were covered in a dark red liquid. Next to my red fingers, I saw the bright, white moon. On the floor? My brain couldn't make sense of it.

How is the moon on the floor? Oh. Stupid. It's a reflection. The moon is reflecting in the puddle of my blood. Idiot…wait…give me a break, I'm dying.

I tickled the reflection with my finger, and it started to glow. I mean, really glow.

What the hell? Another confused thought of a woman seconds from death. *How am I not dead yet?*

I wished it would just happen. Just get it over with. Let me die. But the glowing. I couldn't stop looking at it. The moon in my blood. Glowing brighter and brighter and brighter. Then… I could swear it had just gone into my fingers.

Yes. It had.

My whole hand was glowing. I watched in what I assumed to be a delirium as the moonlight danced through the veins on the back of my hand and up my bare, blood covered arm. Then I couldn't see it anymore; I could feel it. Ice cold. Everywhere. Across my collar bone, down my chest where I could suddenly feel ice around the heat of my open stab wound and a sudden gasp of air rushing into my throat. It felt incredible. It felt as though I had just inhaled the universe. Light and goodness and happiness all in one breath.

 "Don't let this feeling end," I begged as I gazed up at the moon, still and graceful in the sky above me. And then it ended. An almighty, silver light pooled into my eyes and I was blinded.

And that's when I died.

Chapter Two

When I opened my eyes, I was in my bed, staring into the eyes of my fluffy, brown teddy bear, the one with the big red bow – a present from James after our first drug bust. *A nightmare then?* I'd thought.

As I peered through my bedraggled hair, I could see that the day shining through the window seemed just as normal as any other. The sun was shining, the birds were singing. I could hear children on summer break, screaming and playing on the street. I sat up and looked down at myself in my pyjamas. No blood. I felt the skin on my chest. No wound. No evidence of anything.

I tried to retrace my steps in my head. I'd left the gym, I'd sealed the padlock, put the key behind the rock, I'd gone to my car and I was looking for my car keys… then I couldn't stop seeing that nightmare series of events.

The figure... the knife... the blood... the moon... the tree... the light... then nothing...But none of those things could have happened, could they? How had I gotten home and what had happened after I locked those shutters? I sat up further and scanned my room. I couldn't see my gym bag anywhere and I couldn't see my gym clothes. I lifted a hand to my head and stroked my hair. It was dry now, but it was freshly washed. It didn't have the usual layer of grease, the tell-tale sign of a sweaty workout. I definitely didn't remember taking a shower.

I took myself to the bathroom and splashed cold water on my face, taking a deep breath before I looked into the mirror. I didn't look half bad. My eyes looked a brighter green than usual – more alert. My skin, though still smattered with freckles, was brighter and a creamy white as opposed to pasty white. My hair was… well, my hair was still as frizzy as it ever was, but fuller and more vibrant somehow. Not everything was bad. The nightmare hadn't appeared to have affected my sleep. In fact, how many hours had I slept? I couldn't remember how I got home, let alone what time I went to bed.

I shuffled my feet back to the bedroom and picked up my phone. The time flashed up: 09:33.

"Balls," I muttered. Late for work.

I grabbed an orange on my way out the door, but the poor thing exploded in my hand. I looked down at my juice-covered shirt and decided it must have been off, but not as off as the sergeant would be if I arrived late to another briefing. I closed the door and hopped into my car, entirely missing the splatter of blood on the back of the wing mirror.

When I arrived an hour late, the precinct was bustling with life. New recruits were being shown around, fellow constables were gathered around the coffee machine waiting for their morning fuel, administration staff were tap, tap, tapping away as I skulked through the main foyer, trying to cover the orange juice stain from my shirt. Across the way, waiting for me with coffee in hand, was James. Looking gorgeous as ever.

He gave me a wide-eyed grin as he took in my face as though he'd never seen me before. "You look…fresh this morning."

Fresh? Not beautiful. Not breath-taking… fresh.

I smiled nonetheless and felt my cheeks blush. I took the coffee from him and sipped it, trying not to gasp when the liquid hit my tongue. It tasted amazing. I moaned a little too loudly and James took an embarrassed look around to see if anyone had heard.

"What did you put in this coffee?" I gushed.

James shrugged. "It's just vending machine coffee, Loz." I looked down into the cup, half expecting it to be gold.

"You're late," he grunted. "Thought you might be too sore after yesterday's sparring, but I see your lip looks fine."

Now that was another thing. He'd bust my lip last night. Well, I'd bit it, but his punch had made me bite it. I lifted my finger towards my mouth and felt the smooth skin. There was no wound. Odd. Maybe it wasn't as bad as I thought it was. James was still looking at me with the same expression he'd had when I'd walked in. He was trying to figure out what I'd done differently. I wondered the same thing.

Maybe this is what not worrying about drug dealers and gangs does for your skin? I thought. One good night's sleep and James was practically drooling. *Good to know.*

I could suddenly smell a sickeningly dusky aftershave, the familiar scent of Lynx. An aftershave that a Chief Inspector we'd been working with for the last few months wears.

I wrinkled my nose and laughed. "DCI Rowlands is here then?" I joked. James looked behind his back as though Rowlands was behind him.

"How do you know?"

I looked around and couldn't see him anywhere. I frowned. "Can't you smell that? His aftershave?"

James shook his head. He caught something out of the corner of his eye and turned towards the doors across the foyer. I turned to see DCI Rowlands, a large man with slicked back greying hair and a red face, walking through the revolving doors. He was a good distance away.

James laughed and pushed my arm playfully. "Funny. Did you see him in the car park?" He chuckled to himself and made a joke. Something about DCI Rowlands using the aftershave to hide his smoking habit from his wife.

I laughed, though I hadn't really paid much attention to what he'd said as the smell was now overwhelming. I covered my nose. "Seriously. How is that not bothering you?"

James realised that I wasn't joking. I had, indeed, smelled Rowlands Lynx aftershave from before he'd entered the building. "I can't smell anything… Loz, is this your way of telling me your pregnant?" I scowled at him.

"You have to have sex to get pregnant." I shot back, half joking half hoping. He didn't notice, but instead rolled his eyes and lightly punched me in the arm. I rolled my eyes back.

"If you're looking for a volunteer, I'm always available." James and I both turned around to see Richards and Marley. We'd been in the foxholes together a few times and, other than James, they were the two people I was closest to. Richards had come across as sarcastic and a jobsworth when I'd first met him, I frequently wanted to break his nose, but over time I came to like that about him. He used humour as a defence mechanism…I've always had a soft spot for that. Marley, a five foot nothing, curly blonde haired, doll looking girl, had started six months after me. She'd been afraid of her own shadow and I'd frequently questioned why she'd ever joined the force to begin with. That was until I'd worked a night shift with her and had seen first-hand how talented her communication skills were. She genuinely cared. Sometimes that's all people are looking for. Somebody who cares. I'd taken a few hits to protect her, sure, but I never minded. She was my favourite kind of coward. The kind of coward who would sooner heal the world with words than with violence. At this station, she was a wide-eyed lamb, surrounded by lions. Richards and Marley were a couple. A peculiar couple, you may think. James and I may or may not have had a hand in that. What can I say? Opposites attract.

Marley smiled up broadly at me, her pearly whites glistening under the florescent lights. "You gonna let him talk to me like that?" I jabbed at her. She just shrugged. "It's funny that you think I have a say in the matter." She laughed. Richards rolled his sky-blue eyes and pulled a box of doughnuts from behind his back. "Not to be cliché or anything." My eyes must have expressed something resembling a dog being teased with a bone, because they started laughing at me. "I skipped breakfast, what do you want from me?" I whined. Richards lifted the lid off the doughnuts and I grabbed one with pink icing on top, biting into it and, once again, moaning in delight as the intense sweetness passed my lips. I didn't even realise I'd closed my eyes until I opened them again to find all three of them staring at me. "Loz." James murmured with judgement.

"What?" I snapped. He shook his head. Richards laughed deeply. Marley followed, her sweet laugh filling the foyer, earning us a few side glances. "Don't you ever feed her?" Marley chuckled to James. James shook his head by way of response.

"You sure you're not pregnant?" I scowled at him.

"Quit while you're still alive, my friend." Richards patted James on the shoulder.

"She is actually." Marley whispered to the group. "It's mine." She winked at me and I laughed, the tension broken.

"Come on, you geek. Let's go in." I gestured to the office room doors.

"Oh God." Marley pegged her nose. "Is this a long brief? My sinuses can't take the aroma that is DCI Rowlands." James led the way. I followed him into the meeting room where police officers from various departments and various ranks were discussing a six-month-long plan to bust a local gang. The raid would take place tonight at approximately nine O'clock. A time we were certain a drop would be made between Carl Taylor, one of the local drug dealers, and his supplier, a man we only know as Mr. Lorde. Original, I know. The plan was to break down the doors, take the dealer into custody, take the supplier into custody and press some verbal pressure points until someone said something that would lead to the name of

Mr. Lorde's supplier. You see, Mr. Lorde, or whoever he may actually be, gets his gear from somewhere, and we already knew he wasn't the one smuggling it over the border. That's the guy we wanted. The guy who brings kilograms of cocaine onto British land by way of Russian Cargo Ships.

Rowlands walked into the meeting room and silence fell as he took his place in front of an interactive white board with a layout of Carl Taylor's home, on it. A pit of excitement had formed in my stomach. I loved these things. All anticipation that months of planning would finally see action. Action that I would get to be in on. Right at the heart of it all. Tonight, would be the night. All geared up and ready take anyone down who tried to run. Me and James would be positioned at the side door, the door any runners were most likely to escape through. It was our job to prevent this from happening.

Richards and Marley, who's heads I could see animatedly whispering to each other in the far corner, would be out on the front with the first team to gain entry to the property. Richards turned around and gave me an excited thumbs up. I returned the gesture and mouthed, "let's do this." Richards nodded and turned his attention back to Marley, who I could see was seeking emotional support to calm her nerves regarding the impending bust.

I snuck a look up at James as we leaned against the back wall, half expecting to see his hard concentration face, the one that made his jaw line look like it could cut glass. I loved that face. But he was already looking straight at me, his brow furrowed.

He shook his head. "I can't put my finger on it," he whispered. It sounded to me as though he was shouting in my ear, but nobody else seemed to hear him. Goosebumps shivered up my neck. I held my breath without realising. "There's something different about you," he murmured. I didn't know how to respond at first, but internally slapped myself as I remembered how easy James was to talk to and how if I was going to say anything to anyone, he would be the one. So, I tried the truth. "I don't understand it either." I leaned towards him so our arms were touching and stood on my tiptoes so I could whisper in his ear. "I had this dream." I sounded crazy and I knew it. "This… I think it was a dream. I was coming out of the gym and I'd gone to get in my car and then this figure, this shadow came behind me and the next thing I knew I had a dagger in my chest. This… wavy… weird dagger. I woke under that yellow blossom tree and a full moon in a pool of my own blood, and it was all very Teen Wolf for a minute and then there was this light and I woke up in my bed and everything had changed, and I feel weird and I don't know. I just…It's just…"

James rested his hand on my forearm to steady me as I'd suddenly started to shake. "Just what?"

I paused to take a deep breath. "I don't remember getting home, James…" I took another deep breath before I decided to jump on board the crazy train to Crazy Land. "I don't think it was a dream."

"Is there something you'd like to add, PC Smith? PC Clarke?"

I snapped my head to the front of the room. DCI Rowlands stood with his hands on his hips like an irritated primary school teacher. I hadn't realised how loud we'd gotten, or how close. James' hands had somehow become intertwined with mine and our close proximity raised eyebrows. I heard a snigger and could tell by the pitch, it was Marley. I side stepped to put a metres space between James and I.

"No, Sir."

Rowlands nodded his head and turned to face the board where he finished up his briefing on entry and exit points. Richards and Marley exchanged a smirk before turning their attention back to Rowlands. They surely knew my position in this relationship and I liked to think they were rooting for us to take the plunge. The meeting droned on and I lost focus several more times.

When I finally plucked up the courage to look at James again, he was already looking at me, concerned. I smiled to let him know I was okay, and he smiled back, albeit weakly. The lights flicked on and the meeting dispersed in the usual manner; a few rushed out in desperate need of the toilet, a few more for a smoke, one or two stumbled out, bleary eyed and in need of caffeine, and the remaining bunch asked questions and tried to brown nose their way to a fast-track promotion. I hung by the back wall until James patted me forward and we trailed along behind the bleary eyed, followed by Richards and Marley.

Stepping outside the precinct for some fresh air had made me feel the way one feels after stepping out of a cinema after a midday showing – it's always off putting when it's still day light.

 Richards had gone across the car park to smoke and though Marley didn't approve, she accompanied him all the same. I watched them walk away as I cracked my neck and dug my fists into my back to stretch out my muscles. I could see James in my periphery and even without too much effort I could tell he had a concerned expression on his face, his furrowed stare boring into me. It irritated me.

"I get it," I snapped. "You think I'm insane and I should just go home and sleep it off but I can't and I won't. We have the big bust tonight and I'm not missing out."

"I think you need to get checked out by a doctor," he replied, as a matter of fact.

"Thanks mate," I snarled.

"No." He walked closer to me and I scowled. "You were a little bit dazed last night. I clocked you pretty hard. In fact, I probably should've stayed to lock up myself and driven you home. Let me see."

As he reached his hand out to touch my face, I saw my opportunity to shut him up. He hadn't hit me quite as hard as he thought he had, and I felt insulted and annoyed that he saw me as such a weak bodied little girl.

I grabbed his wrist, twisted my head underneath his arm and spun around until his shoulder twisted behind him, then I kicked the back of his knee and forced him to buckle to the floor. I had him pinned, his arm behind his back in what I knew to be a painful position. A few people around us gasped and I could tell they were deciding whether or not to intervene. I internally advised them not to.

"Lauren, what the hell?" he cried out. Lauren, not Loz. Good we're taking me seriously. I leaned in so he could hear me, from behind him, but the now very curious onlookers, couldn't. "You're not quite as strong as you think you are, Jamie. My head is fine. Something more is going on here and I'm scared okay."

My voice broke and it annoyed me even further. A tear ran down my cheek and I wiped it away as I released my hold on him. He slowly picked himself up off the floor and took a few steps towards me.

In the distance I could see Richards and Marley making their way back over to investigate the disturbance.

I wiped my face and looked up, whispering, "I feel like I'm on edge. I can smell things from across the car park, my skin feels like someone's breathing down my neck all the time, I can literally see the sign on the wall of the corner shop right at the other end of the street, I can even tell you the tiny numbers on the chip shop next to it that I've never been able to read before, when we've been driving by. I look different. I feel...honestly, I feel like I'm in the Twilight Zone. It's insane. I'm not even looking right now and I can tell Marley and Richards just stopped. Marley is tying her shoe lace. Now she's walking again. She just tripped." I stared into James' eyes as I tried to will him to see that this wasn't normal. He had seen all I had described as I commentated without watching.

The tears were streaming now. I was standing outside the station, in my uniform, with everyone staring at me and I was crying. Really crying. James pulled me into a hug to hide my face and slowly walked me across the car park, before sitting me in the front seat of his white, BMW.

"What's going on, is she okay?" Richards called over. The couple stopped by the car. I could hear James trying to whisper to them.

"She's just not feeling well. I'm going to take her for a drive, I think, maybe grab something other than fried dough to eat."

"Damn. They were four for a pound. Do you think they could've been off?" Richards mumbled.

I tried to hide my face from them as James climbed in beside me and we sat in silence watching as Marley and Richards walked away, back to the station. The sun was strong today and shone through his car windows with a ferocity. I pulled the seatbelt buckle round. There were a few strings of loose thread that I always played with when I was in his car and wanted something to focus on. I started braiding the pieces together and chewing my lip.

I looked up a few times whenever I heard somebody laugh outside, or a car door slammed shut. I really just wanted him to say something. The silence was starting to feel heavy. I suspected he wanted me to speak first and offer up some kind of rational explanation for my behaviour, however, I felt like being an impertinent child and so continued playing with the pieces of string and sulked until he took the hint that I wasn't going to be the one to break the vow of silence he'd bestowed upon his car. I peeked sideways through a loose strand of my hair. James was watching my hands braid his frayed seatbelt. I tried to figure out if he was lost in his own thought, fascinated by my braiding skills, or just getting a little irritated that I was making the fraying worse. He finally cleared his throat, ready to talk.

"I'm sorry, if I made you feel like I wasn't listening to you. I heard you. I just…now don't get mad again, but I was just trying to bring logic to the conversation in the hope that it would calm you down and maybe clear things up. I mean, let's face is, a concussion is a damned lot easier to wrap your head round than… what? Someone stabbing you to death, except you didn't die and now you have superpowers?"

 He finished, breathing heavy from his mediocre apology. I nodded my head while I tried to come up with a response. Everything he'd said had made sense. Why was I so emotional? It was so unlike me. Maybe he *had* hit me that hard. I sometimes find it hard to accept my limitations and I had felt the world spin a bit on impact. Maybe I'd fallen to sleep, with a concussion, and I had some short-term memory loss. He was right. That was more feasible than anything my brain was currently coming up with to make sense of the nightmare.
 "God."

I laughed and put my hands over my face. My cheeks started to flush from the embarrassment of my outburst. I rubbed my eyes until they hurt. "I'm so sorry. You're right. God, you're right. I'm overtired and concussed. You're right."

James chuckled. "Can I get that in writing please, because, I know I'm right, you are concussed. There's no way you would ever tell me I'm right three times in a sentence if you weren't otherwise mentally impaired." He reached into his car door and pulled out a Kit-Kat. He handed it over to me and I tore into it grateful that he'd been joking about trying to supply me with "real food."

"Thanks, James."

"Any time, Loz. Always around to put you on the straight and narrow when you think you're turning into a vampire."

"I was actually considering it as a viable option."

"God help us all. I've seen you eat. Could you imagine *that appetite* on a blood junkie?" He lightly punched my arm as I gulped down the last part of the melted Kit-Kat bar.

"It's all this sexy energy I'm packing. I need the extra fuel." James smiled warmly at me and nodded by way of response.

"Loz?" he asked, softly.

"James?" I replied, in a mocking tone, though there was a seriousness in his face that made my stomach lurch.

"If I tell you something, don't take it the wrong way." My stomach was doing backflips.

"Okay."

"I really want you to teach me that move you just pulled on me." I internally thumped myself on the nose.

"Will do James. Will do." I could teach you a few other moves as well, if you wanted. Another internal thump for that internal thought. He coughed again.

"You made that seat belt so much worse than it was, by the way." Ah, that *was* what he was thinking.

Chapter Three

The night was clear as per the week prior. It was warm and the summer months were uncharacteristically summery for the UK. Cats prowled the streets like they owned them, and children threw their ball into Mr. Thorp's garden and dared each other to climb into his rose bushes to retrieve it, quickly, before he came out with his carving knife to pop it like he'd warned he would.

I loved nights like this. Although I complained about the heat, these were the nights when people really lived. Moods were always elevated. Drunks from the beer gardens played up and caused an issue, but for the most part, things were settled. Children played in the streets, instead of playing on their phones. Teenagers were out causing mischief and enjoying their youth instead of sitting inside watching TV. The ones who were my age would be out hiking or absorbing the rays in a garden, reading a book (when they're not in full police uniform), and the elderly would meet their remaining living friends in the retirement gardens to catch up and reminisce about the good old days when housing was affordable and wages met the cost of living. These were the nights you remembered.

Unfortunately for Carl Taylor, it was the perfect night to arrest some bad people.

The only issue that came with summer nights was the daylight. It ruined the mood of a good bust. Things became very exposed and the element of surprise had to be planned to perfection. These things actually seldom took place in the dark. If there *were* any runaways, they're easier to track down in the light. Though there were to be no runaways tonight. James and I were, after all, in charge of preventing such an event. We had about three or four more hours of visible daylight. I actually welcomed the setting sun. The weather had been sticky lately and jobs like this were unbearable for a red haired, fair skinned woman like me. I loved the summer nights, where bats roamed wild and free in the sky and you could sit out on a car bonnet, overlooking glorious views from the right spot, sipping lemonade and star watching. All the best memories I had were on summer nights. The night Sensei Clarke had told me I wouldn't be going back into foster care was a summer night. The night James had first told me I was beautiful, well, that had been a spring night actually, but it was still unseasonably warm.

That had actually been a drunken slip on his part. We'd been to a fancy-dress party and I'd gone as Jessica Rabbit, partly because she was the sexiest redhead I could think of (I didn't relish the idea of wearing a wig) and partially because I knew she was James' obsession. I'd met him there and he'd already had too many shots. I'd walked in and bought him a water to help sober him up. That's when he'd said it. Or something along the lines of, "Jess, you look very beautiful tonight." Come to think of it, I don't suppose that counts as him telling *me*, I'm beautiful. I take what I can get. I turned my thoughts to the task at hand.

There was a narrow path towards the side door and I held my breath as I knelt beside it, not daring to move a muscle in case my location was given away. James was tucked behind a potted bush that I couldn't name if you paid me. The bush sat next to the gate – the only exit remaining - as the rest of the squad were in the process of tiptoeing and ducking their way around the perimeter of the house. Not a particularly large house either. Certainly not for a dealer of this magnitude. Although, I imagined that was the point of doing the drops here; it was low key. I spared a thought for Marley and Richards, hoping they would both be okay and uninjured at the end of it all. I shook myself. They'll be fine.

Just as our surveillance team had said, Mr. Lorde was already inside. The transaction was taking place, and as soon as our guys near the front window got a clear view of some illegal substances, it was show time.

My back was dripping with sweat and I could practically hear my heart beating through my chest. The adrenaline was coursing through me at an insane rate. I lived for that feeling.

The wall I leaned against was a tanned, bumpy sort of brick. I rolled my sleeves up and leaned into it. The roughness imprinted on my flesh. I looked up and saw the burgundy wood panelling underneath the gutters, just below where the roof started. It was an end terrace. I wondered what it'd be like to have these people as neighbours. Would it be a nuisance? I guessed it depended on the kind of thing you wanted from a neighbourhood. I certainly wouldn't want to raise my children here, if I ever decided to have them, but for a single woman, maybe someone who didn't face conflict and violence every day, I'd most likely enjoy the excitement of having impending drug busts all the time. I shook away the thought and tried to focus...again.

I turned slightly, careful not to lose my balance, and made eye contact with James. He was watching me, as always. He looked cool and collected, but I knew he was melting as much as I was. He winked and my heart fluttered.

"Moving in," came the voice of our sergeant in my ear. I nodded at James and he nodded back as he shifted onto the balls of his feet in anticipation. I heard the team breaking into the house with the force of a small army. I heard a loud voice yelling. Richards' voice. "Stop where you are! Down on the ground! I said stop where you are!" That sounded promising. They were making a run for it. The thought had barely entered my mind as the side door swung open and a skinny, shaved head, goateed Carl Taylor tried to make a swift getaway. My eyes caught the glisten of silver and my throat tightened as I registered the long sharp knife in his grasp. He moved fast. The only problem for Carl was that I was so much faster than he was. The poor boy hadn't even crossed the threshold before I'd grabbed his wrist, swept my foot into the back of his legs and sent him tumbling to the ground, where I'd cuffed him, pulled the knife from his hand, threw it across the yard and waited for a group of heavily armoured police officers to come and assist. No one else followed. In place of the cavalry was the sound of gun shots. Someone had a gun and it wasn't us. My brain returned to Richards and Marley, and bile rose in my throat as I resisted the urge to run in and check on them. Carl tried wriggling away.

I took several steps back, dragging him with me. He grunted on the floor and spat obscenities my way. My skin felt like someone had poured oil over it and my stomach twisted into a pit of nausea. I held my breath, waiting for more noises. There had been so many shots. That had to be more than one person. How come nobody had realised that? We'd had officers scouting this place for weeks, Richards and Marley had covered several of those surveillance stakeouts; there's no way anybody would have missed that many people. Carl struggled against me again and I looked into his eyes, scowling, daring him to make a move so I could put his face through a wall. Of course, it would take a lot of effort on his part for me to be warranted to do so.

It was one thing to cuff someone who'd bore a weapon and another entirely to allow them to die after you'd disarmed and cuffed them. As much as I wanted to ram my foot down the idiot's jugular, he was in my care now. I sat him up against the wall and put my arm up against his throat. I saw James in the corner of my eye, itching to run over, but he had to maintain his position. There was a series of commands coming through the earpiece, mostly warnings of a firearm.

"You stay there or I'll taser you," I snarled into Carl's face. I inwardly cursed myself for my lack of professionalism but he got me so riled. He stared at me wide eyed, desperately wanting to say something, but being surprisingly smart enough to stay quiet. He nodded sharply and I lowered my arm.

I'd barely swapped kneeling knees to avoid getting too stiff when another update came through. "Lorde's heading to the side door – three officers injured – requiring backup." Another twist in my stomach as I internally prayed the injured weren't Marley and Richards.

A shadow appeared in the doorway. Show time.

Mr. Lorde, or whatever his name was, darted out the door, his tall, muscular figure leaping over the step onto the narrow path where he saw me knelt in front of his handcuffed accomplice. I held my palms to him as he pointed a small gun in my face. I could see it in his eyes, a million thoughts swimming through that calculating brain of his as he realised the part he played, and the part Carl Taylor played. He made his mind up in a second and must have decided Carl was a liability. Better he and his loose lips not be left alone with us for any prolonged period of time. He turned the gun on his partner.

Stupidly, I decided to get in the way. I heard a loud bang and felt a burning sensation in the left of my stomach as I stood in front of that stupid boy. James lunged out from behind the bush, orders be damned, and threw himself at Lorde. The gun sounded again as they hit the floor, the bullet imbedding itself into the wall beside my head. The whole thing seemed to be in slow motion as I realised who had the upper hand.

Lorde had James pinned to the ground. He had the gun pressed into James' forehead and his hand wrapped around his throat.

I was still standing where I'd been shot. The pain had subsided entirely, and I could feel something cold as ice swirling through my veins. I felt powerful. And pissed off.

Mr. Lorde had barely seen me twitch before I had my hand around the barrel of the gun that he'd had pressed into the skull of my best friend. The closest thing I had to family. He pulled the trigger and the gun backfired into his hand, sending a spray of blood over the three of us. James scrambled backwards, feeling his head, half expecting the blood to be his. Lorde was screaming and grabbing his wrist.

Rage spread through me like a forest fire, spreading to every ounce of my being, and I grabbed the little weasel by the collar of what I could finally see to be a very expensive looking suit, and I lifted him into the air. With the ease of swatting a fly, I threw him down the narrow path, where he crashed through the gate, and landed in a heap on the floor. A swarm of officers piled on top of him, patting him down for the weapon that I could now see crumpled on the floor. My heart sang for a brief moment as I saw Richards dark hair and Marley's blonde curls, dive into the fray. They weren't hurt.

"Holy sh--!" I turned towards Carl, who hadn't moved an inch, and was staring at me with something between fear and admiration...or something else I couldn't quite make out. He tilted his head as I looked down at my hands, expecting there to be some kind of answer to where I'd just found that much strength. He sniffed and I looked back up at him. "What drugs are you on, girl?"

"I – I don't...I don't do drugs," I garbled out between ragged breaths. I looked down at my hands again. The world seemed brighter and more vivid, as I entered into a state of shock. I didn't even see James move, but there he was, standing in front of me. He'd lowered me to the ground for some reason and was shouting for help.

Why are you shouting for help? I'm fine. I thought.

He was frantic. "Help! Help!" he screamed towards the officers.

Someone ran in, I wasn't really sure who, and knelt beside me. There was a mess around as they removed my vest. Through my periphery, I could see Richards and Marley rushing over and stopping sharply, looking down at me. "Take him." James snapped, pointing to Carl.

"Was she hurt?" Marley asked, a quiver in her voice.

"Take him." James repeated, with a warmer tone.

Richards moved first and Marley followed, grabbing Carl and dragging him across the yard, through the destroyed gate, as I lay and wondered if Mr. Lorde would have people who could take care of him in case he blabbed. Someone lifted my shirt and there was a pause in action and a deafening silence.

"Is this a joke?" A medic snapped at James. Reality came back to me in a rush. James only stared at my stomach, a very confused expression on his face. The medic tutted and stormed off, leaving a nice view of the sky. A plane flew across. I wondered where they were going. Or maybe they were flying home from a family holiday. How nice would that be? To have a life so settled and mundane that you had to find pleasure in a distant land. Screaming children on water slides, mosquito bites and pre-vacation vaccinations to protect you from Hepatitis B and C and whatever else. I wondered idly as I could feel James run his hand across my stomach, if he would ever fancy a holiday away with me? Just as friends. Where would we go?

"Where would you go, if you could go anywhere in the world, James?" He didn't answer my question but continued his examination of my stomach. "James… what on earth is wrong with you?" I tried looking forward.

"Loz…" he whispered. He lifted his hand to show me the blood and a whimper escaped my lips. Oh God. When did that happen? "How bad is it?"

"You were shot." It came back to me as the last of the adrenaline cleared from my mind. The gunshot and the cold feeling. I nodded and swallowed back a lump in my throat.

"Of course I was. I know. I felt it. Funny, the things we forget."

"I saw it. I saw the gun go off, I saw it hit you, I saw the blood."

"James, I know." A tear ran sideways into my hair. "How bad is it? It must be the adrenaline; I can't feel a thing."

I remembered I had hands and put them on my bare tummy. I felt something wet. When I lifted my hand, there was blood on my fingertips.

"Oh God," I cried. "Where'd the medic go?"

I tried to look around, but James suddenly stood me up in one smooth move and half pinning me to the wall, he used his sleeve to wipe the blood off my stomach.

"Look! Look at it," he whispered frantically. I looked down at my stomach and saw... well... nothing. There was nothing. No hole, no pouring blood, no gunshot wound to brag about at all.

He lifted his sleeve to show me the blood. "This is yours. Your blood. From a gunshot wound I *saw* you get."

He looked down at the floor, and his face went a funny shade. He bent down and picked something up. As he opened his palm to show me, I nearly threw up. A bullet.

Curled up as though it had hit something solid, it was covered in blood. His eyes lifted to meet mine and a mutual understanding sparked between us. James' hand shook and the next words to come out of his mouth were barely audible.

"Loz…"

He lifted Lorde's gun from the side of his belt, where he'd tucked it away. Looking at it now, I could see why the gun had backfired. The barrel had been crushed and there were fingerprints around the crushed area.

"You did that. You bent the gun. And when it backfired, it practically exploded his hand but yours is fine. You picked that guy up like he was a bag of icing sugar and threw him through a wooden gate like a car had driven through it."

I couldn't tell if he was scared for me or excited. There was something I'd never heard from him before, a tone I couldn't name and an emotion my brain wouldn't compute. His eyes were almost brimming with tears and I kept looking around to make sure we weren't being listened to. There was a lot of activity in the house, a lot of people being arrested, and I noted vaguely that the tactical unit had arrived. They were faster than usual. The thing is, nobody was bothered by us and this was a good thing as I suspected James was moments away from either an exciting realisation or a mental breakdown. He gripped my arm and my stomach lurched at the warmth of his hand. Even amongst all the craziness and the sheer unbelievability of what was happening, the smallest touch from him was the most thrilling thing.

"It's okay James."

"Is it okay?" he asked, his breathing irregular. "How are you so calm right now? You got shot...and you healed...Loz..."

I looked into his eyes, trying to find words to respond, but nothing came. I didn't know why I felt so calm. Something was happening, that much I could sense. It felt... familiar. It felt normal. My main concern was James. A suppressed laugh escaped his throat as he looked around to see if anyone was listening. Everyone was busy and paid us no notice.

A bubble of anticipation worked its way into my chest as I allowed James' excitements to contaminate me. I stopped caring about what was happening with the raid. Something far more interesting was going on right here. James grabbed my arm and pulled me further up the path, so we weren't in anyone's earshot.

"I think we need to go back to the gym and see what's under that blossom tree."

Chapter Four

Getting away from work wasn't easy. James had reluctantly bagged the gun as evidence but had pocketed the bullet that I'd been shot with.

There were questions being asked about what had happened. Marley had found us shortly after we emerged from the yard and caught us up, after double checking I was uninjured of course. If only she knew.

Apparently, Carl Taylor had a group of men living with him, acting as bodyguards. They had all been armed and opened fire when our team had moved in. Everyone had been too distracted in the crossfire to assist with anything going on in our allocated spot at the side of the house. This was actually fortunate, as it gave us the opportunity to cover up my bloodied shirt and ditch the vest with the bullet hole under the shed. Taylor was being put in the back of a van, saying nothing the whole time while a crumpled Mr. Lorde was being seen to by the medic who'd thought we were wasting his time. No doubt someone would be back to go over the property, but we had time before then to move the vest.

My brain was practically buzzing with thoughts. I'd seen all the superhero films, I knew how I was supposed to feel about this. I was supposed to be outraged that I couldn't be a normal girl, annoyed at my newfound duty to use my powers for good, etc etc etc, blah, blah, blah. Don't get me wrong, I'd certainly been weirded out that morning, but in light of the fact I'd just expelled a bullet from my abdomen, healed entirely and thrown a man twice my size through a wooden gate, I was feeling pretty great about the whole thing. I just didn't understand how it had happened. James was right. We had to go back to where it all started.

When we were back at the station, we typed up our reports in record time, fed the DCI some bull about having to follow up on a tip relating to a series of catalytic converter thefts we'd been working on, entirely avoid Richards and Marley, lest they have questions, and jumped in James' car at the first opportunity.
 When we arrived at the gym, it was around nine in the evening and the car park was about as busy as it had been last night.
James pulled into the far corner, right in front of the yellow blossom tree. I sat in the car staring up as the petals fell, hypnotising in their beauty. The night was getting cooler as the sun started its decent behind the surrounding hills, it was a welcome change from the heat that had made the car insufferable to be in. We got out and wasted no time in climbing over the greenery, which

was a mistake as the events of last night had, unsurprisingly now, *actually happened* and we had just stepped straight into a dried-up puddle of blood. My blood. A funny noise escaped my throat and James reached out to steady me as I swayed. We took a few steps to the side, dragging our shoes across the grass in an attempt to rub the sticky blood off.

"Oh my God," James breathed. "It actually happened."

I sat on the floor by the crimson stain and allowed the blossom to rain over me. I looked up, half expecting the full moon to be beaming its light onto me. There was an empty space of navy blue, the moon not having risen above the hills yet.

I closed my eyes and let cool air sooth my freckled face. I needed a minute to think.

Okay. It happened. It really happened. But how did it happen? Why?

I felt James' presence as he leaned over me. I slowly opened my eyes and saw his quizzical face watching mine. He held out his hand to help me up.

"I'm trying very hard not to freak out right now," I whispered. James nodded.

"Tell me about it."

"Yet you're still here." I looked up at him. He smiled.

"Like I'd ever leave you. Besides, I've always wanted to be in a horror film. Believe me...as freaky as this is, I'm getting a major kick out of it."

I smiled weakly. "Glad you're having fun." I grabbed his still outstretched hand and he lifted me off the floor in one clean move. James looked around, searching for clues that weren't there, until he realised, we had the best clue of all.

"Loz?"

"Uh-huh?" I looked at him and he pointed towards the gym. I turned around and smiled.

"Brilliant."

There were CCTV cameras on every corner of the roof, and one was staring right at us.

Tony Marquess was the broadest northerner you could ever meet. He was a large fellow, with bulging muscles, no neck, tattoos up either arm, and that typical northern hospitality charm, you hear about so often. He also happened to be an old school friend of Sensei Clarke, James' father. All of this came in very useful that night, as when we'd sheepishly requested we see the footage from last night, after telling him a complete lie about someone putting a nail in my tyre, he'd swung open the office door, set up the cameras playback on his computer and brought us two steaming cups of coffee. "I'll leave yer to it." Tony had said before taking himself out of the room to give us some privacy. I secretly thought he was rooting for James and me to give it a shot. I secretly thought *everybody* was rooting for James and me to give it a shot.

James sat beside me, leaning towards the computer screen as we skipped through until we saw Tony leaving. The room was small and the desk was messy. There was a half-finished can of lemonade next to a half-eaten cheeseburger. I felt guilty for disturbing Tony's meal. I knew his wife, seldom let him eat fast foods and wondered if he'd be internally seething that he'd left this in here with us. A pack of matches made me wonder if he'd been secretly smoking as well, but I smiled to myself when I saw there was an oil lamp in the corner and a meditation guide pinned on the wall.

I wriggled in the chair, trying to give James some space. His arm was pushing against mine and I could smell his aftershave. Definitely the right amount of Lynx. Not too much at all. My tongue felt thicker in my mouth and my heart started beating faster as I looked at his lips through the corner of my eye. I wondered what it would be like to kiss him. I internally slapped myself. Someone should throw iced water on me.

Everything felt different today, like my skin was electric. I was sensitive to everything. I guessed my attraction to

James was just on overload right now. Just like everything else.

"There."

I snapped my attention back to the task at hand. James was pointing to an image of himself getting into his car and driving away. I followed shortly afterwards and hid the key as usual. That's when we both saw it. The figure. A woman. She had long black hair, but we couldn't see her face. She pulled up her hood as she rounded the corner and made a beeline for me next to my car. I spun around and the next events happened so fast, we had to slow down the playback speed. She knocked my bag to the side and snaked forwards, plunging the dagger into my chest. I had to look away. James gave my hand a gentle squeeze. I could feel his racing pulse and his palms clamming with sweat. He had started to shake.

"She's dragging you behind the bush," he said, his voice barely recognizable. I looked back to the screen.

"Who is she?" I whispered. She really had just left me for dead. The woman ran to a barbed fence separating the gym's car park from an industrial estate, and she leaped over in exactly one fluid jump. She landed on the other side as smoothly as a cat, before prowling off camera.

"Did you see that?" I breathed.

James nodded, slowly.

Although my body was slightly obscured by the blossom tree, we could still make out some movements. My hand had lifted, and then a pause and suddenly a glow. We zoomed in, just to be sure, but it was undeniable. My hand glowed. Then, as it dimmed, we could see a faint white light, spread across my body. We couldn't see much more after that, and the screen went blank.

After a moment, the camera cleared up as the light darkened and we saw that, somehow, I had stood up. My back was fully erect. I was standing unusually straight and was looking up. At the moon perhaps?

Then... I started to take my clothes off. Mmm... nice and awkward...

Mostly because, instead of saying something along the lines of "Oh Loz, you're so beautiful, wow, you're an exquisite creature," James had spun around in his chair, turned his back to the screen and held up his hand to cover his eyes. "Oh God, turn it off." Not exactly the reaction a girl wants when her lifelong crush sees her naked for the first time. I, however, thought I looked pretty darn good.

There was an orange flash that I'd missed at first, but when I played it backwards, I nearly laughed in a I'm-going-to-need-therapy-after-this kind of way.

"Erm. James?"

"What?" he said, his back still turned. I spun the chair around, forcing him to watch, as I replayed the last five seconds.

Unsurprisingly, given how the past twelve hours had gone, me stripping naked under the moonlight wasn't the most surprising thing to happen. We had to replay it six times at different speeds to fully understand what we were seeing. I had wondered where my clothes had gone. Surely, if I'd have found my bloodied gym gear sooner, I may have been able to draw a more accurate conclusion of what was reality and what was nightmare, a lot sooner. There was no way I could have found my gym gear, however, because according to the CCTV footage, from that night, I had incinerated them with my bare hands.

We watched, mouths open, as ash spilled from my hands, I picked up my gym bag from the side of the road, jumped in my car and drove away. James leaned forwards and hit the pause button. He cleared his throat and wiped sweat from his neck, before turning to look at me dead in the eyes.

"And you don't remember any of that?"

"Nothing."

I leaned back in my chair as a weird thumping started in my head. James leaned forward, and I watched as he picked up my hand in his. My breathing stopped as he traced his fingers over my palm. The hairs on the back of my neck stood on end and a pit of butterflies opened in my stomach. Such a small thing like that had never bothered me so much before. I was so much more sensitive to everything. To James above all else.

"So strange," he mumbled. "Do you think you could do it again?"

I shrugged in response while I swallowed, trying to open my throat again. He leaned back, mirroring my stance.

"Maybe, the woman was from some government agency? Maybe they've been watching you and were interested. Is it possible, that the thing she stabbed you with, hadn't been just a knife, but something imbedded with a serum of some kind that gave you these… is powers too corny a word? Gifts? I don't know… abilities?"

"Abilities works," I agreed.

"Is that too far-fetched an idea?" I laughed at the ridiculousness of his question. I stood, leaning over the computer and restarted the clip.

"Shall we just watch this again a few more hundred times before we start playing hard and fast with the term 'far-fetched?' No, it's not. It's not a bad idea at all, in fact, it's the most logical idea I've heard all day."

James raised his hands in submission. He looked around a moment, then grabbed a book of matches off the side. He pulled out six, before pulling me over to sit down and placing them in my hand.

"Just try," he whispered.

I looked at the matches and laughed. "I have no idea how I did that. I can't remember anything."

"You didn't know you could throw Mr. Lorde the way you did, but you did it anyway. I don't think this thing is as complicated as learning how to put on the four-figure restraint. I think it's instinctual. At the raid you saw me in trouble, you saw my life was in danger and something took over you. I saw it."

"You saw that?"

"Course I saw it. Something animalistic came over you. It looked so natural. When you got shot, no one taught you how to heal yourself, your body just did it. So, try not trying." His hand slid underneath mine and he pulled his chair closer, so our knees were leaning against each other. "Let instinct guide you."

I looked down at the matches in my hand. I felt his skin on mine. His knees touching mine. His gaze was mine. My only instinct was to kiss him. My eyes looked towards the matches and saw past them. They saw his hand, holding mine. I looked up and he was already staring at me. Our eyes locked. Those deep brown eyes.

"Let instinct take over," he whispered. Was I affecting him the way he affected me? He leaned in closer. I could feel his breath on my mouth. Our gazes still held each other's. It was surprising how calm I felt. I could hear my heartbeat, steady and strong. A cold rush ran across my skin and my insides felt like ice. I couldn't stop looking at him. His eyes had changed colour somehow. They were now a golden, almost orange, flickering, burning… Then I realised as I looked down at the palm of my hand. The matches were on fire. My whole hand was on fire.

"Woah." James wheeled his chair back. "That's… woah."

The flames were tickling around my flesh. I could feel the warmth, but no pain. It wasn't immediately obvious where the source was coming from. The fire just seemed to be there. My sleeves had rolled down and started to catch fire. The white started to char, and I let the matches drop into a bin and James poured a can of Lemonade over it and then my sleeves.

The flames around my hand remained. I watched it, mesmerised, and smiled at him. He laughed and ran a hand through his hair. The whole moment was beautiful and crazy, and insane and so, so, incredible. I suddenly forgot all about the previous night's attack and threat on my life. I forgot about everything bad that had ever happened to me. This moment would be etched into my brain for as long as I lived. How could it not? This was magical. There I stood, the girl nobody had wanted, the strange red-haired kid who had screamed at the world when nobody listened. There she stood, creating fire. Fire that made the whole room glow. An experience that silenced the chatter of my best friend. A gift that made him laugh in excitement. I looked up at him and I thought his smile would split his face.

"You're amazing," he gushed. A warmth filled me. I opened my mouth to say something, but even I wasn't sure what it would be.

Suddenly, the door flew open and the flames disappeared. Tony stood in the doorway, holding up his phone.

"You guys might want to get back to the station. I just had a phone call from a friend. There's been an attack. Some woman stormed the place. There're no details yet, but the whole station had to be evacuated because of some sort of gas."

James and I looked at each other, aghast. We'd turned our radios down when we started searching through the footage but as we turned them up again a series of requests started buzzing through – all urgent – none negotiable. All on duty officers were to return to the station. That boded well. It meant the supposed gas was probably not deadly or they'd have kept us all away. The threat must have been eliminated if we were being called back.

I clicked off the footage and took Tony back to his desktop of a koala in a palm tree. Cute.

"Did you find what you were looking for?" Tony asked. James smirked at me and I replied, "Sure did," before we raced off out of the office. I heard Tony sniffing dramatically and then he called after us: "Hey! Have you kids been smoking in here?"

Chapter Five

When we arrived at the station, everyone was hanging around in groups around the car park. We ditched the car and tried to mingle with a few colleagues to get a picture of what had happened as Fire Fighters made their way into the building. I scanned the crowd looking for Richards and Marley, but they were nowhere to be seen. I spotted a woman I knew from CID. She had short brown hair and a short temper, from what I'd heard, though all I'd ever experienced was the kind of attitude that gets you ahead in life. Strong will and a thick skin. I really liked her and we'd actually had a few laughs in line to the coffee shop around the corner.

"What happened, Lisa?" I asked as James joined the fray. Lisa seemed excited that she'd been called upon to give us the gossip. Her eyes sparkled as she relayed the series of events that had led us to this moment.

"From what Chris told me, you know, the really fit guy from forensics, he told me that he saw some woman storm through a fire exit, like she owned the place, and headed straight for the Custody Suite. He'd tried to ask her what her intention was and received a back hand for his efforts. A backhand, that sent him flying into a group of newbies. They loved the action, I think. Anyway, this sets off alarm bells from everyone who saw what had happened and a bunch of people from all over the place came to help. Lauren, I'd never seen anything like it, I swear I was shaking. I wanted to give the cow a punch myself, you know what I'm like, but I was shaking. No one could handle her. Anyways, she literally headed straight to that guy they brought in this morning; you know the one?"

"Lorde?" James asked, irritated by her ramblings.

"Nah, not the supplier, the other one. The one with the goatee."

"Taylor?" I asked, incredulously. Lisa nodded her head in an exaggerated way.

"Yeah, that's the one, the drug dealer." James looked at me, one eyebrow raised.

"What did she want with him?" I asked. Lisa shook her head in an overexaggerated way.

"Lauren, that's not even the scary bit. That's not the bit that really got me shaking."

"Well, what was?" James snapped. Lisa raised an eyebrow and I really didn't have the time to mediate an argument.

"He's just really anxious, we went through a lot bringing Carl in." Not a lie in the least. Lisa turned to me and took a deep breath before continuing.

"Right, so this woman goes straight to Carl Taylors holding cell and just as a bunch of other people arrive to stop her, he stands up and, I kid you not Lauren, he puts his hand on the wall and the whole cell exploded." She shook her head to demonstrate her disbelief.

"Exploded?" Reiterated James.

"Exploded, exploded. The whole damned cell. This woman goes flying across the room and I don't know. It must have been a coincidence, him touching the wall at the same time as the explosion. They think it was a gas leak. But still. Weird timing. It was just chaos."

"Where's Carl Taylor?" I asked, anxiously.

"Oh, they got him, don't worry about that. The woman tried running but she collapsed before she made it across the car park, so they took her into custody and I think they've gone to hospital with her now, getting her checked out. Your mates copped for that job."

"Richards and Marley?" I asked. She nodded. That's where they'd gotten to.

"So why are we still standing around?" asked James.

"Because," Lisa said, as though it was perfectly obvious, "they have to check the gas mains for a leak. They don't know what caused the explosion for sure. I want to know how that Taylor guy got off without a scratch." James and I looked at each other. "It's a good job it happened when it did though, that woman had motives, to kill him, I think. They confiscated this really weird knife off her."

My stomach sank. The world swam in front of my eyes as

that night's events spun in my mind for the millionth time. Surely not that knife.

James asked the question before I had chance. "What kind of knife?"

"It had a wavy blade, these weird markings on it and when they actually had a good look, they think it's made from rock, with a kind of glaze over it."

I took off running back towards the station. The ground hit my feet at a speed I'd never achieved before, my muscles felt no burning and my lungs did not tire to pull in the right amount of air. I could hear James struggling to catch up with me. I was through the station doors before DCI Rowlands, who had been stood with a fireman, had a chance to call out my name. I disregarded his orders to stop. I headed straight to the evidence lockers and paced around, though I had no idea what I was really searching for. A few minutes later, James flew through the door, panting and clammy.

"You can outrun me now? I'll have to remember that. Jesus. I can taste blood." He leaned against the nearest locker to catch his breath. "Loz, it might not even be in here."

"It's here." I didn't know how I knew; I just knew. I tried to pay attention to the way I felt as I walked past each locker. James watched me intently. As I passed a locker with a peace sticker, half ripped off, in the centre, the hairs on my arms stood on end. I placed my palm over the metal, and I felt something pulsing.

I grabbed hold of the lock and tore it off, making the locker door fly open. I decided it would be easier to stop being surprised by anything anymore. I was just rolling with it at this point. I couldn't waste time pausing to be astonished by my excelled prowess.

My heart stopped. There it was. In a plastic evidence bag. The knife.

The knife.

Complete with wavy edges and a metal that wasn't a metal.

I took it out and my hands shook. I could see now what Lisa had been talking about. There was a strange symbol, like a triangle, but the lines didn't connect and there were three dots going down the centre. The grey rock was smooth and seemed to have a resin coating.

James leaned over me and rested a hand on my shoulder. "Is that it?"

I nodded. "I want to see her."

I expected him to argue that it wasn't a good idea, but when I looked at him, he silently took the knife from me and slid it in his inside pocket.

DCI Rowlands was waiting for us, incredulous, as we walked out the Evidence locker.

"What the hell are you two playing at?"

"Sorry, Sir," I said with conviction. "I had a panic about the evidence we confiscated from the raid this morning. Had a gut feeling that girl could have been a decoy. You know what these gangs can be like." Rowlands seemed to soften slightly. A dedicated officer, wanting to check in on her case, make sure all was well, and all the ducks were in a row. He nodded his head, once, slowly.

"Good woman." He leaned out and patted my arm. He pointed to me but looked at James. "Got a good one here, haven't you?"

Usually, I would be the first person to correct someone who suggests that I belong to anyone, but now was not the time, so I bit my tongue. Time for the next cover story. "Erm. Who took the intruder to the hospital?" I asked, trying to sound as neutrally uninterested as possible. I of course, already knew the answer, but wanted my next offer to seem spontaneous.

"PC Richards and PC Marley, I believe. Why?"

I nodded my head, pretending to think and then snapped my fingers to suggest the idea had just popped into my head. "You know Sir, they were working last night, I don't think they got finished before three in the morning. Erm, why don't me and PC Clarke head there now and take over. I'm feeling pretty fresh myself, what about you, James?"

"Fresh as a daisy."

Rowlands stuck his bottom lip out in surprise. "Are you sure? Haven't you two been on shift since this morning?"

I elbowed James in the rib, and he nodded enthusiastically. "Full of beans, Sir. Really, we're just… absolutely full of beans."

Rowlands tilted his head and I grew a little anxious that he'd think we were on drugs. If I'm being completely honest, I wasn't entirely sure we hadn't had something slipped to us in our morning coffee. What was in those delicious donuts anyway?

He nodded and I let go of the air I hadn't realised I was holding.

"Sure," he said. "That's very good of you. Tell them I sent you, they can call me if they need to confirm." I stuck my thumb up and we walked, slowly, down the corridor towards the exit.

"Is he watching us?" I asked. James glanced over his shoulder nonchalantly.

"Nope, he was just digging for gold, actually."

I giggled.

A kind nurse showed us to the bay in A&E where PC Richards was standing outside. He seemed different. His face paler and dark circles under his eyes. He swayed where he stood, his eyes surveying the room. "Look alive." I joked and I went to playfully punch him in the arm. He stopped my fist with his hand with a speed and force that send a sharp pain, shooting up my wrist. I cried out a little in shock and forced my hand out of his grasp. "What the hell?" I exclaimed. Richards eyes were passive. I realised they seemed darker than usual. Almost black. His mouth was in a hard straight line and he tilted his head in a way that made me uncomfortable. A shiver ran down my spine and my skin suddenly felt as though oil was running over me. The feeling felt familiar.

"Where's Marley?" I asked, barely a whisper.

"Marley?" Richards whispered back. His voice was his own, but colder.

"Short woman. Love of your life. That Marley." I said, side eyeing James who was looking at Richards in a very quizzical sort of way.

Richards pointed with his thumb to the Bay. James walked in and returned a moment later with PC Marley. She, too, looked paler and exhausted. "Woah guys." I breathed. "You should both go home. Get some sleep. Maybe take a vitamin D or two." Neither moved. James stepped to my side and addressed the pair.

"Have we pissed you off or something? What's wrong with the pair of you?" James laughed uncomfortably at their muted response.

"Okay." I murmured. "You guys stand here looking like you haven't slept in a millennium; I just need to see something." I tried to walk into the bay, but a heavy hand on my stomach stopped me. To my complete shock, it was Marley. The shock wasn't just the force of which she had stopped me, more the scowl she was giving me. This is the girl I'd had to take punches for. This was the girl nobody else wanted to work with because she hated the physical stuff. Yet, she seemed to have no issues getting in my way. "Marley?" I asked. She stared up at me. My stomach felt funny looking into her eyes. It was almost a vacant expression, with a veneer of malice. I looked up at Richards. I noticed neither had given James the time of day. They'd not spared him one glance. If they were mad, they were mad at me. "Have I done something wrong?" They exchanged a glance. Marley removed her hand and looked down at it. She brushed her fingertips together and looked up at me, tilting her head in the way Richards had. She looked back up at her lover. It was like they were having some kind of unspoken conversation. A second later, Marley stepped aside. "Thanks." I mumbled. I turned to James and grabbed his arm. "Come with me?" I asked, though it was more of a command. James nodded and followed me as I walked into the bay.

I took a deep breath and opened the curtain pulled around a bed. A woman lay under a think blue blanket with her back turned to us. Both of her wrists were handcuffed to the bed.

We approached tenderly. "Jane Doe?" I asked, looking at the whiteboard on the wall. "Guessing that's not actually your name."

I was under no illusion that she was asleep. She was listening to every word. I already knew, looking at her hair, having seen the knife. She was the person who had tried to kill me. The one who had plunged that dagger into my heart, dragged my body behind a bush and left me for dead.

I had a few questions. Not the least of which being: "Did you know what was going to happen to me or did you expect me to die?" She stirred at the sound of my question. Her shoulder tilted back, her hair fell off her face and her eyes starred widely, and wildly, into mine.

If she hadn't tried to end my life, I would have told her that I thought she was beautiful. She had golden brown eyes, almost hazel, with flecks of green and yellow around the iris. I would have put her in her late thirties but suspected she could have been older and just took care of herself. She had olive skin with a sprinkle of dark freckles over her perky nose. Her lips were full and her eyelashes dark and thick. I almost hated her immediately for her natural beauty alone.

The look on her face told me the feeling was mutual. Though, somehow, I don't think she hated me for my beauty. There was a snarl across her mouth and a spark of fear in her eyes.

"Get away from me," she snapped, pulling violently at the handcuffs. James stepped between us, but I moved myself back and leaned in.

"Who are you? Why did you do this to me?"

She froze as she seemed to recognise me for the first time. "I know you… I killed you. Straight in the heart, I didn't miss. I never miss."

"That was a confession if I ever heard one," said James.

"How are you still alive?" she continued.

"Why did you do this to me?" I asked again more forcefully.

"Because it's what I do… and you made a mistake coming to me with that in your pocket." She turned her eyes to James, who took an involuntary step back. "Yeah. I can feel it. The way I can feel *you*. I don't pick and choose my jobs. If I sense what you are, I end you."

I started to wonder if maybe she was a hitwoman but didn't really get a chance to ponder this as she suddenly pulled at her cuffs with such force that they snapped into two. She lunged at me and we tumbled to the ground.

The back of my head smacked the floor and the world spun. She jumped off me and kicked James in the chest. He flew through the curtain and into the side of the nurse's station outside. I pulled myself up in time to see her strut over to James, pull open his side vest pocket and tear out the knife. The nurses and doctors in the area dispersed and I waited with bated breath for Marley and Richards to assist. They were nowhere to be seen. Maybe they'd gone home, I wondered idly, rubbing the back of my head.

The assailant ran at me. I was ready for her and threw my arm out, deflecting the hand which wielded the dagger, I used the bed for a peg up and flung my legs around her neck, before throwing my body weight to the floor and wrestling as I pinned her and tried to pull the weapon from her hand at the same time. She managed to break free from my hold by punching me in the back with an agonising force. As soon as she had the space, she pulled me up by my shirt, threw me against the wall and, just as she aimed and plunged the dagger forward, I reached out in a blur of speed and grabbed the wavy blade.

A loud ring pierced my ears.

Her eyes widened in shock and I took my chance, twisting the blade between my hands until it crumbled to dust with a grotesque sounding crunch. Through the corner of my eye I saw, who I thought to be Richards, standing in the doorway. An intimidating shadow. The ringing still echoed in my ears and everything slowed down. I turned and looked at Richards. He stared at me. Through me. Into me. His eyes protruding. He glanced down at the crumbled dagger then bore his eyes into mine. A sickening feeling swept over me. A shifting in front of me returned my focus to the danger before me and using her bodyweight, I lifted myself up and kicked my attacker in the stomach. She hit the wall across the room and she slid to the floor, revealing the cracks her body had made in the plaster. I turned my head to the doorway and Richards was gone. In his place I saw James approaching as he rushed over to be by my side...I didn't need any help. The woman's eyes had remained open the whole time. Her mouth hung down and she panted as she tried to catch her breath. I was ready for her to come back fighting. I was ready for her to run. I was not ready for what she did next.

Tears flowing down her face, she began to laugh. Not a laugh from telling a funny joke or from seeing someone fall, but a laugh, not dissimilar to finishing a marathon after months of training. Delirious, uncontrolled, erratic. She laughed and laughed as the tears continued to flow.

James looked at me and I looked back, shrugging my shoulders. She didn't stand, but instead threw herself forward onto her knees, looking up at me in what now seemed like admiration.

"It's you. It's you. It's you. Finally. After all this time. It's you." She bowed her head to the floor and her palms slid towards me as though she would touch me but dared not do so.

"Erm… Who am I?" I asked, leaning down.

The woman sat up, staring at the crumbled dagger on the floor. "*What brings her life will turn to dust if it ever tried to do her harm…* I thought it meant your mother or your father… It meant the weapon. That's the problem with these prophecies… They're open to interpretation." She spoke with awe but frankly I was a little creeped out.

"Come again?"

"I'm so sorry. It's… It's the prophecy. We've been waiting for you for millennia. This was always how it was supposed to happen. You had to die to be reborn… I just… I didn't realise at the time. You have to understand. It's instinct. We just kill what our instincts tell us holds Erebus' energy. I thought that's what I felt, but it must have been something else."

My brain hurt.

"I have no idea what you're talking about." I was starting to feel sorry for this obviously crazy woman. She stood up with a speed that made both me and James step back until our backs hit the wall.

"Please," she said. "I won't hurt you. Either of you. Please give me a chance to explain. I know you're confused. I know you are. Please, try to trust me."

I scoffed.

"Trust you? You stabbed me in the heart. Literally!"

She nodded. "Yes, I did, but look at me. Because those instincts must be coming to you now. Knowing when someone is standing behind you, feeling connections that you didn't feel before. Listen to it. Listen to your intuition. It trusts me. It *has* to."

Actually, I hated to admit it, but I did. I couldn't explain it. I shook my head. "You're insane."

"I'll prove it. You agree that there's something happening right now. Something you can't explain?"

I shrugged my shoulders.

"Things are happening to you," she continued. "Things that don't make sense right now. You're stronger, you can hear more, smell more, see more. You're possibly showing abilities that are not of the world you know. If I'm right then please, take my hand. You'll feel it. I know you'll feel it."

I stepped forward slightly but James pulled me back. "Are you insane?"

I couldn't stop looking at her eyes. Those beautiful eyes. I could feel them burning into mine, begging me to reach out.

So, I did.

I took her hand and felt a warmth and familiarity I'd never felt before. It came close to how I felt when I found out Sensei Clarke was taking me in. Close to how I felt whenever James stood beside me. I could have handed this woman a gun, had her hold it to my head and I would have trusted her not to pull the trigger. I dropped her hand with a jolt, but the connection remained. I looked at James and nodded, ignoring his pleading eyes.

"It's okay." I whispered. The woman stepped closer and blinked back tears.

"See," she smiled. "I'm Deborah Price…but everyone calls me Debbie."

"Lauren… he calls me Loz, but you can call me Lauren."

"James," James grunted, waving an unenthusiastic hand and shaking his head at me. Debbie smiled at us.

"Lauren, James, will you please come with me? I have a lot to show you and it would be my honour to shed some light onto what a confusing twenty-four hours this must have been for you both."

"You don't know the half of it." James said.

"Actually, I do. Follow me… Did you come in a car? Great. It's a bit of a drive to my house."

"Your house?" James chuckled. "Really? You think they're going to let you leave? Let alone that we'd take you anywhere."

I pulled him closer to me so I could whisper in his ear. "James, I know. I know, okay? Please, I can't explain it. I can't explain anything, but I trust her. I trust her, okay? And if it turns out to be a trick, I'll kill her myself. But we're in way over our heads and I believe her when she says she can make sense of any of this."

He cupped my chin and lifted my head to meet his eyes. "I don't trust her."

"Good. I know you'll have my back." He dropped my chin and stepped back, throwing daggers at Debbie. He pointed out to the staff who had crowded around the opposite side of the room in fear of the violence that had just taken place. "All good!" I called out. Debbie tapped his vest, where his police logo sat.

"They'll let you take me anywhere."

"Mmm," he said. "That's right." Sometimes we forget we're in uniform. He shook his head for the millionth time and looked me dead in the eyes before resigning to his fate and spinning around with a winning smile on his face. "Just going to step out for some fresh air," he shouted out to the nurses.

Chapter Six

"I wonder where them two went." James said as we stepped outside.

"Which two?" Debbie enquired.

"The other two officers who brought you here. Richards and Marley." Debbie tilted her head quizzically and furrowed her brow. "There *were* two others you're right...I...I almost forgot." She rubbed at her temple. "Woah. It's been a long night."

We put Debbie in the back of the Police car for the drive. Even though my newly found instincts told me to trust her, I was happy to be separated by reinforced glass. We could still hear her, which was both a good and a bad thing. It was good in the sense we could ask questions; it was bad in the sense that Debbie snored.

 I've always found it fascinating when people can sleep in public spaces. I'm always too on edge for that. Not Debbie. No, she was doing just fine. After mumbling about how her fighting skills were genetic and then something vague about how I would be much more impressive once I reached my peak, she had fallen asleep. This can't have been more than a half hour after we'd gone on the motorway. I tried rousing her, for a more detailed explanation, but she'd passed out.

I let James drive so that I could think. What had just happened? I was finding it hard to ask any more eloquent questions. The bizarreness of the past day was too complicated to even contemplate making sense of alone. I didn't really have much of a choice, except to go wherever this Debbie was taking us and hope to find answers at the end of the road.

The trees sped by and cities in the distance became smaller towns, the further we drove. According to the Sat Nav, we had fifteen minutes left on the journey. We'd turned the radios off and had essentially gone AWOL. We knew we'd be in a world of trouble when we returned, and I had no idea how we would explain this away. Though, I was sure Marley and Richards would cover for us for as long as they could. Hopefully enough time for us to get some distance. As far as outside appearances were concerned, we'd kidnapped somebody in police custody. Nausea swept over me as one thought bounced to the next. Why did Richards and Marley act the way they did? Where was Debbie taking us? Or, should I say, where were we taking her? What am I? Alien? Vampire? Shapeshifter? Witch? Not human, that's for sure. Unless the whole government experiment thing was actually the truth. Was Debbie leading us into a government facility where I'll be poked and prodded until I agree to do their bidding? Lauren the super spy...has a nice ring to it. I felt

James' hand hold mine, by my lap. I squeezed back, afraid that if I didn't do it tight enough, he would disappear. I couldn't believe he was still here. Following behind me on my crazy journey. He had nothing to do with any of this. His life had been turned upside-down because of me. Tears filled my eyes. I wiped them away before they could fall down my cheek so he wouldn't see. He saw. We both know he saw, but he said nothing about it, nonetheless.

"Go home." I said, barely above a whisper.

"I'm not going anywhere," he whispered back. "Not ever, I promise." He squeezed my hand again then returned to the wheel.

I sniffled back my secret sorrow and turned to him. "How are you so calm? It's like you were built for this. I'm pretending to be calm, but I'm completely freaking out inside.

James shook his head. "Calm? Loz, my heart has been beating out of rhythm since you walked into work this morning. I knew something was off, but this?" He shook his head again and a pang of guilt stabbed my chest.

"I'm so sorry, for all of this. We're gonna be in so much trouble. If anything happens to you, I swear I don't know what I'll do."

"Hey, nothing's going to happen to me."

"James, she kicked you clean across the room. I'm not afraid for my life anymore. I'm afraid for yours."

Silence. I wondered if I had offended him somehow. Perhaps he was embarrassed at how easily he had his arse handed to him. He cleared his throat.

"She killed you, Loz… and I don't care that there is a world out there that I clearly know nothing about. I don't care if it turns out you're some long-prophesized queen who'll lead the world to salvation. We're family." He stopped whispering. "I love you. I've always loved you. I'll always love you and even if you grow a second head and five arms that shoot arrows, and I stay the same, I'll still throw myself into the line of fire to save you… I'm with you."

My head was reeling with the words *I love you.* Did he mean he loved me like a sister? That would make things awkward but would make a lot of sense. I didn't want to ask. I didn't want that kind of humiliation on top of everything else going on, and he had essentially just told me he would die for me, so I'd say that's a strong place to leave the topic.

Before I'd had chance to come up with something funny or sarcastic to say, Debbie made us both jump by calling through the glass, "Pull off here."

We pulled into a car dealership, with lots of balloons and a ten-foot-tall, inflatable green man waving in the wind. It reminded me of a horror film I'd seen recently. It had a white panelled roof, with four white beams reaching down to the floor - the underneath looked very basic. Bricks and windows.

I had a nosey at the cars in the lot. They were separated into four-wheeled-drives, hybrids, electric, automatic and manual – as per the sign on the side of the building. The prices in the large SUV vehicles they had at the front of the lot, (probably as a draw to people with money) seemed quite fair and I pushed away the thought of taking one for a test drive.

James turned off the engine and we both turned around. Debbie was leaning her forehead on the separating glass and watching us.

"Are you kidding?" I asked. It was coming up for two in the morning and we'd been awake for too many hours. My eyes were stinging, I hadn't eaten since the chocolate bar James had force fed me that morning in the station car park, my feet were sore, everything was weird and confusing, and I really was *not* in the mood for games.

"I need you to let me out," Debbie said, leaning her forehead on the glass and wiping sleep out of her eye. She looked between us and realised we weren't budging. "We need to ditch this car because, by now, someone will know I'm missing, and they'll have thought to track this vehicle, and there'll be people on their way for us. I'd say we have about ten minutes to get a head start in a fresh pair of wheels, before they catch up. If we don't move

76

before then, then I'll have to escape and it's going to be so much harder to do that with the two of you. So, c'mon." She pulled at the door handle. "I have to pee."

At first, I thought she was full of it. After all, what kind of a car dealership is open at two in the morning? But, as I'd scrutinised the building, I saw a light on inside and the shadow of a person move by the blinds. With any luck they'd tell her she couldn't use the toilet and we'd be back on the road in a car the police could track. I knew Richards and Marley would realise by now that something was off. Probably when they came back to Debbie's bed to find it empty and James and I missing. They'd think to check the tracking but hopefully, instead of raising the alarm, I hoped they'd come themselves. This way, I could explain everything to them directly. It seemed the best way to keep us out of trouble and to still get the answers I needed.

James and I waited outside whilst Debbie went in to use the bathroom. The night was cooler than the past nights had been, and the moon hung high in the sky. I stared into the craters on its surface. I felt a deep connection, a sense of knowing and familiarity that tickled a distant memory that I couldn't quite unlock.

Despite the coolness that the night brought, there was still a stickiness that wouldn't go away. The air still felt heavy. I was desperate for a little bit of rainfall, perhaps even a hint of thunder to clear the humidity. James leant against the wall. The gutter above shielded him from the moonlight. A shame, I thought, as it had made the blonde highlights in his otherwise brown hair stand out and turned his eyes a haunting black when he looked towards the horizon.

 "She's not what I expected," I said as I leaned against the wall beside him. He didn't look at me but smirked to himself.

 "What?" I asked.

 "Nothing," he said, still smiling. I laughed in an irritated sort of way. "Don't just say *nothing,* then carry on smiling. What's so funny? You do realise we're following this woman around like lost puppies. We have no idea where we're going, we're probably going to get fired after this possibly worse. And above all else, yesterday I got stabbed in the heart and today I'm setting fire to my hands and throwing fully grown men in the air… so please do tell me, what's so bloody funny?"

 "Finished?" He said, amused. I just shrugged, trying to remain serious. "All of that is what's so funny. This woman thought she'd killed you. Now she looks like she'd kill *for* you. And, if I'm being frank, I think you kind of like it. All this excitement. The mystery. You're thriving, I can tell."

"I know you saw me cry. Don't tell me I'm enjoying myself, because I'm not."

He shook his head. "No, not enjoying yourself. You can thrive in an environment and not enjoy it. Look at soldiers who can't adapt back into regular society after touring war zones. Do you understand what I'm saying?"

"Mmm. Yeah. Not that I like to admit it. I get you. I hate when you make sense after I've already disagreed with you." I slouched down to the floor and James slouched beside me.

"Of course – we can't ever admit that I'm right about something." I looked at him and reconsidered my second joke of the day.

"You're right about lots of things." His response was one of mock shock.

Debbie emerged with a rucksack in her hand and a set of keys. She was followed by a middle-aged man with greying brown hair, grey eyes and muscles that could probably pop the head off a rhino.

"Erm, hello," I said as I stood up.

"Sorry. He wanted to see you." Debbie looked at me sheepishly and tilted her head towards the man. "This is Amos. He's an old friend of the family. Amos. she's not going to understand what you do. We haven't gotten around to all that yet."

Amos waved her off. "I'm not going to keep you. I just wanted to see your face. If you ever need anything, my dear, you come straight here. I'll help you."

I looked to Debbie for some kind of hint as to how I was supposed to respond. She shrugged.

"Will do," I smiled at Amos. He seemed thrilled enough.

Debbie beckoned us to follow her and we headed straight towards a Range Rover that had been pulled around the front. Amos watched, his eyes seeming to glimmer as we walked away from him. I imagined this was what it must be like to be a child waving goodbye to a grandfather after a visit. I waved and he waved back. I decided I liked Amos.

"Take your jackets off and anything else that identifies you as police," Debbie instructed. James hesitated at first, then took off his vest and utility belt. I followed suit. Debbie opened the rucksack and took out a pair of jeans and a shirt, handed them to James, then pulled out another pair of jeans and a plain white crop top for me. "I don't have any shoes for you, so you'll have to keep your boots on. Sorry."

"Where did these come from?" I asked. "Who was that guy?"

"Get in the car, get changed and I'll explain."

James shook his head. "No. We're moving too fast. Tell us now. Then we *might* get in the car."

I was grateful for that. I went along with the flow too often and, although I was strong headed, I could sometimes be a bit of a pushover. James, however, would question everything. We used that way of thinking in our job roles every day. Good cop, bad cop. Cliché, but a recognized, tried and tested technique.

Debbie sighed. "Amos is like me, but I'll explain that when we get to my place, in a lot more detail. He's semi-retired from his field, but he's kind of a stop point for other people like us. He's the go-to when you're in a pickle. He'll provide transport, a place to sleep, food, clothing, weapons. Whatever you need, really. Now can you please get in the car?"

"Weapons?" James asked.

Debbie pulled a dagger out of the rucksack. I took a step back. It was identical to the one I'd crushed.

"Relax," she said. Seeing my reaction, she put it back in the bag. "I would never hurt you again. Ever. I'd be killing myself and everyone else if I dared. Even if I wanted to, this wouldn't be the weapon to work. Believe me." James snorted derisively. Debbie opened the back door and beckoned us to climb in. "I'm pretty sure I can hear sirens, we have less than five minutes to get ahead of them before it becomes a problem."

James frowned. "I can't hear anything."

"I can," I said. He looked at me blankly for a moment, then nodded.

"Who am I to disagree with a woman and her superpowers?"

"Who indeed?" Debbie chuckled.

My heart sank as I realised Richards and Marley had to have reported us. I guess even the closest of friends can put their jobs above loyalty. I decided I'd have to try very hard not to take it personally. I mean, really, if the roles were reversed, I'd probably do the same.

We climbed into the Range Rover, and instantly felt incredibly thankful for the car's air conditioning. Debbie jumped into the driver's seat and buckled up, tapping another postcode into the Sat Nav.

"Ooh, almost forgot," she said, reaching a hand into the rucksack. She pulled out three burgers and passed two of them back to us. "Amos heated these up for us."

I expected James to decline, but he hadn't eaten since breakfast the previous day, and jumped at the chance for something substantial.

"I'm starving, thanks."

Debbie smiled back at him. "You're welcome." She turned to me and flicked her long dark hair from her shoulder. "He's warming up to me."

"Way to a man's heart is through his stomach," I replied, considering how I could, somehow, joke with such ease with a woman who had tried to end my life not twenty-four hours ago.

She pulled away from the dealership onto a gravelled backroad. James had finished his burger and was staring at the back of Debbie's head. I elbowed him in the side and winked.

She scared him.

Chapter Seven

After being on the road for an hour, we approached a Travelodge.

"We should stop here." I just shook my head.

"It's been a long day for everyone," she continued. "We're not going to make it any further. I need to sleep. You need to sleep. Please."

James looked at me. "We could take turns keeping watch," he suggested. There were little pillows under his eyes. I nodded in submission.

I felt like I could probably argue my point further, but then reminded myself that the only reason he was even here was because of me. None of this had anything to do with him at all. In fact, I wondered what I'd done to deserve such a loyal best friend. I looked again at his eyes. He was so tired. My heart twisted with an uncomfortable sympathy and I nodded.

"Fine."

He smiled weakly at me, knowing I was anxious to reach some clarity. I was probably also in need of some sleep and was comforted by the fact I still felt human in that regard… and that Debbie wasn't as invincible as I'd thought. We were all on common ground for the first time. Best had get some rest.

Checking in took about ten minutes. We booked for one room. We didn't trust Debbie to be left alone. James took first watch, Debbie took the pull-out sofa and I snuggled into the double bed, resting my head on James' shoulder. He provided an element of security so that I could relax and let sleep take me.

We swapped shifts two more times that I could remember, but when I awoke next, the sun was high in the sky. My phone showed it was already one in the afternoon, with no missed calls or text messages from Marley or Richards. Was that a good sign?

Someone knocked on the door.

James was asleep beside me and I realised Debbie was gone. I sprang from the bed, shaking James awake.

There was another knock.

James shot up and I went to the door. I opened it slowly and Debbie pushed past, carrying a tray of coffees and a bag of food. "We need to get going. I let you guys sleep as long as I dared but really…we really have to go." James looked around like he wasn't sure what had just happened, but my faith in Debbie shot up a little more. She'd had many opportunities while we slept to either kill us or leave us and here she was, offering coffee and food to the guards who'd fallen asleep on duty.

We checked out and hit the road pretty soon after that. We'd kept the window down to save us from the sauna we now rode in, given the high positioning of the sun. I'm not sure how long the journey took from there, but I was finding it extremely difficult to stay awake, despite my long rest. I wondered if it had been something to do with the changes my body was going through. I didn't fight the next wave of exhaustion as it took over and I closed my eyes.

When I awoke, I had my head rested on James' shoulder. I noticed, blearily, that he'd taken my boots off. I sat up, rubbing my eyes a little too aggressively.

"Sorry," I mumbled.

"You're okay," he said. There was a croak in his voice and his eyes were bloodshot.

"Do you want to get your head down for a bit?"

He shook his head. "We're only ten minutes away."

I peered out the window. The sun wasn't far above the horizon. I'd probably been asleep for hours. *Where is this place?*

As though she had read my mind, Debbie explained, "We're not as far away as you may think. I've been driving erratically in circles to make sure no one was following us. It's an irritating necessity."

We seemed to be in the countryside. I took out my phone and found I had no signal. I gently elbowed James and showed him. He nodded slightly and showed me his phone, which he already had in his hand, so I could see that he also had no signal.

A few more minutes passed in silence and I suddenly caught sight of a house in the distance.

A big house.

Ginormous actually.

The closer we got to Debbie's home, the more evident its grandeur became. The whole building was a reddish brown, with a grand black roof and brilliant green vines climbing around the perimeter. The windows were Georgian and black. I counted twelve on each of the three floors and a large square glass box, like a conservatory without the frames, carved into the left side of the roof.

The tyres crunched as they rolled over a gravelled driveway and we turned around a fountain before stopping outside a double black door, between two white, vine covered columns. I pressed my nose against the car window.

"Wow," I breathed.

"This is your home?" James gasped.

Debbie climbed out of the car, taking her rucksack with her and walked around the doors, opening them one by one to allow us out. I stepped out with just my socks on my feet, holding my boots in my right hand. With my left hand, I held onto the bottom of James' shirt, like a child crossing a busy road.

Debbie looked at me with shining eyes. She had been all business, abrupt and pushy, but now we were apparently safe, *that* face had returned. She seemed almost shy, as though she wanted my approval. She needed me to like her home.

"It's been in my family for many generations. Renovated hundreds of times over the years. It was built on top of a crater, over two thousand years ago. A crater, caused by an asteroid." She looked at me, pointedly, as she said this, as though it was supposed to mean something to me. If anything, I was confused.

"How is that possible?"

"How *is* it?" she replied, a smile on her face.

I shrugged. I had no idea. "It's beautiful, regardless." I said, hoping to pacify her expectations that I'd somehow understand the meaning of everything she said. She smiled widely and my heart hummed that such a small gesture could make somebody so happy.

The black double doors were opened by the largest man I had ever seen. He was pure muscle and looked like he could kill me with the swish of his gigantic hands. I knew instantly that he was Debbie's father. He had the same black hair and the same magnificent eyes. He swept her up into a large bear hug, lifting her feet off the ground and spinning her in three wide circles, before setting her softly on the ground.

He then turned his looming frame to James and me. James grabbed my hand as if this was supposed to stop this man from picking me up as well...it didn't stop him at all.

He grabbed the two of us with one arm and lifted us off the ground. My face squished against the crisp white shirt he wore, and I could smell his cologne. He laughed, and I could feel it deep within his chest.

James' hand was clammy, and I kept having to readjust my grip so he wouldn't let go. The giant lowered us back onto the ground and stepped back to take us all in. Debbie stepped to the side, beaming.

"Lauren, James, this is my father, Marcus. Father, this is James, and *this* is Lauren." She looked up at Marcus and her eyes filled with tears again. To my complete and utter shock, so did Marcus's. He wiped them away with a meaty sausage finger.

"Amos called to let me know you were coming. I can't begin to express how honoured and unbelievably blessed I feel to have seen you in my lifetime. There are trying times ahead of us all." He put his hand on Debbie's shoulder. "But there's time for all of that. Please, make yourself at home. What's ours is yours. How long do you expect you'll be staying with us?" I looked at James, hoping he'd have a clue.

He shook his head. "I suppose that depends on what you both have to say about what's happening to Lauren." A fair statement.

Marcus nodded his head sharply and looked down at Debbie. "No time like the present, I suppose," he chuckled. Debbie took a deep breath and gestured for us to follow her inside.

Debbie led us through a black and white tiled hallway and up a grand staircase, with a varnished black wood, banister spiralling in a curve, all the way to the top. I felt like a piece on a chess board in more ways than one.

My eyes couldn't rest. Every step we took offered something new to look at. Down below, as we ascended, I could see black, glossy doors, lining the walls in the hallway. Bunches of roses, in elaborate vases, stood on tall, black tables. When we reached the landing, I discovered it wrapped around the upstairs like a balcony, looking down onto the front door.

We followed Debbie down a long corridor that forked off the landing and seemed to transport us into a completely different kind of décor. A different century, in fact. The walls were cold concrete and had flamed torches hanging on them. The concrete was draped with a long red carpet leading us into a darkness at the end.

I unconsciously reached for James's hand, but realised he had never let go. I leaned in closer to him, instead. He squeezed my hand tighter and I think he felt grateful that I still needed him.

"One sec."

Debbie stopped us at a door and I laughed when I saw the fingerprint entry system attached to the wall. It was so out of place. Right here, in the middle of what seemed to be a medieval torture chamber, there was a state-of-the-art security system on a very weak door.

It swung open, revealing a reinforced steel door behind it. This door slid open with a large metallic clang.

"Another renovation, I suppose?" James asked.

"They built a lot of the house around this. I remember the day this room was built, actually. I was six."

We stepped over the threshold and I released James. My hands instinctively flew to my mouth. I had never seen anything like it.

The whole room was one massive painting. Colours I didn't know the name of glowed across the canvas. I looked under my feet and saw water, depicted with every blue I had ever seen, swirling around in mesmerising circles. Around the edges of the floor, there were flowers of red, yellow, white and indigo. They were clinging to vines and twirled, around, weaved in and out of the water. My eyes couldn't take in the walls.

 I saw a painting of a woman several times along one wall. She seemed to age as I walked beside her. A girl, no more than four years old, with long blonde hair and sky-blue eyes, sat in a village. A black cloud surrounding them. There was a large lake. The girl fell in. The girl was in the village again. Darkness, darker than before. The girl had a white star in her hands and the darkness was gone. Then, on the opposite wall, the girl became a woman. She seemed to be loved by the village people. The darkness returned. I could see a face, with glowing red eyes, coming out of it. The woman was there again. She spoke to the people. There was something that looked like a floating sphere and then what appeared to be an explosion. Then I thought I saw... me. A woman with long red hair, freckles, green eyes.

 "Holy Sh—"

James ran over, having seen what I had. "What the hell?"

 The woman wore the same gym clothes I had worn the night Debbie had attacked me. There was Debbie, wielding the dagger. There I was again, lying in a pool of blood under the moon. The blossom tree floating over me. Another light. Then, further along the wall, I was standing, larger in this image. I wore a long white dress with tears rolling down my cheek.

I stopped breathing when I saw that the rest of the room had gone black.

"What is this?" I breathed.

Debbie was stroking her hand over the image of the night she'd killed me. A tear rolled down her cheek.

"All these years, I had no idea this was me... All these years..."

James gave me a questioning look. He reached out and touched the paper on the wall. I followed suit and saw what he had seen. It was old. The closer I looked, the easier I could see it. The corners near the edges of each image were folding. Someone had gone to great lengths to try and preserve the art, but its age was still coming through.

Then another question crept up on me. "Debbie… how old are you?"

She laughed and wiped away her falling tears. She threw her hands in the air. "Six years older than this room."

I looked around. James asked the question. "How old is this room?"

Debbie smiled, sideways. "Three hundred and twenty-two years old. Making me –"

"Three hundred and twenty-eight," I finished. She smiled and nodded.

"How is that possible?" I asked, trying to hide the quiver in my voice.

Debbie crouched on the floor and looked around. Then, she inhaled deeply, having found the words.

"Let me start by saying: everything you think you know about how this world came to be, is wrong."

Chapter Eight

"Don't get me wrong," Debbie said. "Throughout history, some snippets were heard, and a few things got lost in translation. You may already be familiar with some of what I'm about to tell you, even if you've heard it differently... Does that make any sense?"

"No," James and I said together.

She nodded and thought again before responding. "It's like Chinese whispers, right? One person tells a story, thousands of years ago. The person who hears it tells another story and they tell someone else and so on and eventually person A hears what they told person B, by person X, and person A is like *That's not even close to what I told person B.* And now, there are hundreds of different countries across the planet and they all think they know the story person A told by heart, but actually, person G told one country one version and person J told someone else something different and actually, person A is long dead so nobody has a clue what they're talking about and everyone is trying to fill the gaps using the information given by someone who was never even in the alphabet to begin with. You know? So, eventually, my people just stopped trying to explain to the world what was happening around them and that's how we ended up fighting in the shadows. Protecting everyone from a darkness that nobody even believes in anymore."

My head was starting to hurt.

Debbie stared at our blank expressions. "Okay. I'm going about this all wrong. Why don't I just tell you everything from the beginning and you can make the connections yourself?"

We both nodded.

She took a deep breath and started walking around the room until she reached the picture of the little girl in the village. A look crossed her face of pure serenity as she rested her hand on the painting. She began a story I could tell she had heard a thousand times and had, perhaps, told a thousand more.

"Before this planet came to be, another stood in its place. A planet, called Eden. It was a simple world, and the people were early in their existence. A peaceful people. Villages were small and spread across the globe. There was one village in particular, ran by no one person, but as a collective. The word *violence* was passed by no tongue. Death came only by age. This village was settled by a large lake, the people called *Selene*. It was believed to have been formed by a great explosion. Something we know today as an asteroid. They believed this asteroid created Eden and that they lived by the source of a great entity.

"Lake Selene created a flow of water, which became a creek. The people used this water to grow crops, drink and bathe. Their lives were a paradise and so was Eden. Until one day, a father killed his son over the last piece of fruit on a low hanging tree, and this one act of violence bred. The people soon started to see a black cloud rolling in above them. It formed tentacles and entered into the bodies of the village men and women, using them as vessels. It set Brother on Brother, Mother on Daughter. Other villages started to experience the same kind of possessions and a name rang out across Eden, a name they had given to the darkness. They called it: Erebus." She ran her hand over the darkness on the canvas. "An entity of chaos. It never stayed long, arriving from the sky in spurts. It travelled from person to person, only satisfied when somebody was killed. When the periods of respite had grown shorter and shorter, and it seemed like all hope was lost, the people joined together and prayed to *Selene*. They prayed for her to save them from the darkness, to save them from Erebus.

Not long after, a little village girl called Gaia, a sweet thing of four years, with hair whiter than the sun and eyes like the sky, walked down to the creek alone. She fell in and the fast-flowing waters dragged her little body into the lake.

"Her Mother and Aunt had been praying by the waterfront and saw this happen. The villagers searched the lake for hours and hours, until the sun had set behind the distant mountains and the stars couldn't light their way. Devastated, Gaia's Mother believed she had drowned, and the people believed her to be another victim of Erebus.

"The following morning, to everyone's immense delight, Gaia returned to the village, alive and well. Her dress of wheat hung dry around her small frame. As her mother held her, Gaia whispered something into her ear. A request.

"Her Mother called the people together and Gaia stood before them. A girl who seemed so different to the one who had fallen into the creek. A girl whose eyes appeared older than her face. She told the people to not be afraid, that Eden had spoken to her. The ground, the soil, the water, the life of the planet had resurrected her with a purpose. She told them that Selene had blessed her with gifts and the strength to banish the Erebus. The people believed in her. They had no choice. All other hope had been lost.

"Sure enough, the following night, Erebus returned to take more victims. Gaia, the child though she was, walked through a cloud of darkness and emerged free from the evil influence. She fell to her knees, dug her hands in the ground and pulled from it a ball of light…the soul of Selene. The light engulfed her body and erupted from her palms a beacon. The light carved into the darkness, smothering it and Erebus rebounded, shooting into the sky and back into the Universe from whence it came, banished from Eden.

"The people were so grateful to the little girl. The following morning, they presented Gaia with gifts of flowers, fruit and bread, and after placing a crown of roses upon her head, they made her their Empress. The celebrations lasted weeks.

"Gaia reigned on Eden for millennia, surpassing two thousand years and never aging a day past her twenty-first birthday. Eden was bountiful and Gaia was a kind and gentle ruler.

"It was not to last.

"The darkness returned, having travelled for two thousand years to take revenge on the child. Erebus had grown stronger. He had ravaged other worlds beyond theirs and with every moment of chaos he brought, his strength and body had grown. When the cloud appeared again, sending a shadow of death over Eden, Erebus had a face. Eyes redder than hate and a mouth of fangs it used to engulf the land.

"By this time, the technology of the world had thrived, and Gaia ordered her people to take to the stars, in search of a new home, as far away from Eden as possible. The people were reluctant to leave their beloved ruler and so she made them a promise. She told them she had lived long enough and so had Eden. She said she would destroy this planet, scattering its body, along with herself and Erebus. She promised that, from the destruction, she would form a new world. A world where Selene would watch from above and send warning when the darkness started to emerge from the ashes. This world would be called Earth and would birth warriors born with the strength of Gaia and with the knowledge of what had become of Eden and her people. Warriors with strength and speed and the power to keep Erebus from forming again, using weapons born of Selene's flesh, to not just expel, but destroy pieces of the darkness.

 "But Gaia had her own fear, that her eternal sacrifice would not be enough. So, as her people took to the skies in their worldly shaped ships, she made a promise to Eden. A message she spoke with a conviction the stars would believe. The words of a prophecy to fall on the ears of the future soothsayers of Earth. That one day, a girl would be born from the darkness.

 "This girl would have a false name and she would be the light in a shadow, a warrior of her own making, a guardian of the people. If Erebus's form ever became so great as to threaten the existence of her new world, a sacrifice would be made by the flesh of that which repels the dark.

"Then let it be said that what brings her life will turn to dust if it ever tried to do her harm. And upon her resurrection, Selene and Gaia would meet in her heart, and the girl with the false name would become Theia, the Mother of Mothers, Goddess of Earth, the prophesized Warrior or Warriors, to obliterate Erebus, and she would lead the universe into a new age, free from the darkness, once and for all."

Debbie's cheeks were flushed and her eyes were bright. She looked so full of life. I, however, felt like someone had just put a sledgehammer through my skull. James cleared his throat and I saw him sitting on the floor like a child at story time.

"Why do I feel like I'm being inducted into a cult?"
I kicked him with my bare foot and realised I had lost my boots. I had definitely had them in my hand when I got out of the car.

"I understand your reaction," sighed Debbie. "But find me one fault in what I just told you."

James scoffed. "I wouldn't know where to begin."

"Look, this is going to be a whole lot easier on all of us, if you just say, for argument's sake, you believe what I'm saying is true."

"So… When you said that thing... that thing about the sacrifice..."

Debbie nodded and held her hand over the painting of my death. I noted that she seemed proud of her involvement. I pointed to the image of her wielding the dagger.

"*That*," I said, "is not *flesh*."

Debbie smiled at me. "Actually, it is."

"Come again," James said, walking over to look.

"Do you recall when I said this house was built on a crater? A crater caused by the asteroid of moon rock?"

"Yeah," we said in unison.

"That was the warning the prophecy foretold. Selene sent warning by breaking off a piece of herself and sending it to Earth. We're standing on the start of this planet's first intergalactic war. In fact, this entire planet was created *for* this war! Warriors have been birthed since the dawn of man, with this knowledge genetically branded into our heads, we've always been ready. But two thousand years ago, an astronomer, one of our own, saw a burst of light come from the moon and explode into the Earth. Warriors came from all over the world to gather the moon rock and forged weapons from Selene's flesh. Weapons we knew would destroy the parts of Erebus that would soon start infiltrating societies around the globe. That astronomer was my grandmother many generations back. Our family is known by people like us all over the world."

She had finally reached my limit.

"You're crazy. Oh my God... you're all *crazy*. You're what? Immortal? An intergalactic war? I mean *come on!*"

Debbie continued, seemingly unaware of my tone. "No, we're not immortal at all, actually. Our aging started slowing down a great deal when Celest – that's the soothsayer who painted this room, actually – started having visions of an impending shadow. Our bodies still age... just a little slower. We don't really know why but I suspect it's because the final battle is growing near, and our numbers need to be strong. We can still be killed."

"Soothsayers? Right. Of course. Makes perfect sense."

"They're, to us, like what a religious leader is to you. There is only one in the whole world at any given time. Celest is the oldest there has ever been. She came here from Naples to paint this. Look at it. It's old... You know it's old... and yet she painted you, and me, and that night... before you were even born. Look at it."

I walked away. For a few moments, I held my face in my hands. Then, I looked up.

"Okay," I conceded. "If you'd told me all of this yesterday morning, I would have had you sectioned, but I'll admit...if seeing is believing, then I've seen it. There's no other way I can logically explain everything that has happened over the last twenty-four hours." I turned to James. "Can you?" He didn't respond. "But I just have one more question. If all of this is true... If I'm the one who's going to stop this Erebus, whatever in the hell that really means – then what is this?" I gestured to the black wall and ceiling, then to my large figure. "Why am I crying?"

Surprisingly, the answer came not from Debbie, but from James. "Because the prophecy isn't finished yet." He looked at Debbie for confirmation.

She smiled sadly. "We know you're the one who'll wipe Erebus from existence. We know you'll lead us into a new age. A better one than the last. We just don't know how. No one knows how. It's something to do with Selene and Gaia and Theia. Celeste can't see past Erebus anymore. He's too strong. When she lost the sight, she came here to immortalise the story."

Debbie took the dagger and passed it to me. Gingerly, I took it. "It can't hurt you, remember. We've been fighting a losing war. These daggers are the only thing that can kill the scattered parts of Erebus, but only when it's possessing a host."

"Does the host die?"

I couldn't see how they would survive, so I wasn't shocked to see her nod. I was however outraged. "No."

"No?" She confirmed.

"I'm not killing people." I spat. Debbie shook her head. "You're saying that now but you'll see it first hand, eventually, you'll have to. You'll see that we don't use the word evil lightly when referring to Erebus. This entity ravages the human soul, takes it away and stuffs in its place something dark and twisted and it'll force that human to kill and assault and destroy lives."

"I won't kill a person."

"It's a necessary evil. They're lost to themselves when Erebus infiltrates their mind and we have to weed out as many parts as we can. The more parts that come together, the worse off we are. We know, now, that there is somewhere on this planet, where a host or maybe even a large body of water, contains a substantial amount of his matter. We just don't know where."

"I survived," I jeered. "What's to say that there isn't a way to do what needs to be done, without killing anybody. I mean, what I'm supposed to take what you say at face value but I've never even seen an Erebus. You can't expect me to go around stabbing innocent people with the very blade that killed me – or didn't kill me – or whatever the hell happened to me."

She shook her head. "That was Selene. I have a theory about that. We know that there had to be a sacrifice in order for you to be resurrected. I think the dagger – the moon rock – it entered into your blood stream under the light of a full moon and forged a connection. Selene was able to reach out to you… That's where your power came from. Like she did for Gaia."

"Why did you target me to begin with? Why did you sense Erebus? Was I possessed without knowing?"

James piped up again. "No. You're Loz and you always have been. I would have known if something had changed."

"Not only that, but we, the Warriors, *can't be* possessed by Erebus. You *have* to have warrior blood, because the warriors were birthed from Gaia's body, from the part of the Earth she became when she sacrificed herself, whereas James, you were birthed from the part of Earth made from the bones of Eden. That's what we believe the prophecy refers to when it says Gaia and Selene will meet in your heart. You're a warrior. You're already a part of Gaia."

"But I don't have any of the memories you do," hearing myself joining in on the craziness.

"And that's the darkness… there's something about you. I can sense it. I could sense it last night. Something that hangs around you. Maybe that's why you don't have the memories the rest of us do. I'm sorry, I just don't know how to fill that gap."

I sat down and leaned against the door, my head spinning. I heard a bleep and the door slid open.

Sophisticated as ever, I fell flat on my back. I looked up from the ground and saw Marcus beaming down on me. "Would you like to join us for dinner." I sat up on my elbows and looked towards James for an answer. He shrugged and ran his hand through his hair, in defeat. "I could eat."

Chapter Nine

Marcus led us to two rooms down the black and white hall.

"You should change for dinner," he told us.

I could see that James was apprehensive about leaving me but I waved him goodbye and followed Marcus to the next room.

When he opened the door, I gasped. It was like no bedroom I had ever seen. The room was large and adorned with crimson drapes. There was a four-poster bed made from dark mahogany stained wood and white curtains draped around it. A dressing table, a chest of drawers and a wardrobe, made of the same wood as the bed, were dotted around the walls of the room. White candles created a warm light and a fireplace crackled below a hanging mirror. I looked up at Marcus and he smiled down on me.

"Like it?" he asked. I assumed he already knew my answer.

"I love it," I said, gushing. He patted my head.

"I'm glad. There's a change of clothes for you on the bed. Please, let me know if you need anything else." I thanked him and he saw himself out. I ran to the bed and pulled back the curtains to reveal a golden, sparkly dress.

I picked it up. The fabric didn't feel itchy. It fell through my fingers like silk. I wasn't entirely sure of the material, but I loved the way it felt. I threw my clothes off and pulled the dress over my head. It fastened at the neck and then plunged down the centre of my chest, hugging me in all the right places and flowing out just above the knee.

I looked into the mirror and decided to pull my hair into a bun, pulling down curls at the front. It sat frizzy on top of my head but was still an improvement to wearing it down. I saw, behind me, a pair of strappy gold heels, and realised they had a red bottom. I picked them up and examined them. They were *Christian Louboutin's*.

"You're beautiful," I told them, before slipping them onto my feet. I examined my reflection and nodded myself an approval. "Not bad, kid."

It then occurred to me that we were awfully dressed up. I'd been lost in the sheer beauty of my borrowed clothes. I wondered if everybody else would be as dressed up as me or if this was another show of affection to their prophesized saviour.

In all honesty, I thought they'd made some kind of mistake. I conceded that there was truth to what we'd been told, but I didn't have to concede that I was going to liberate the Universe from an unseen entity that I'd never heard of. There were still so many questions. But in that moment, I was happy to play along and be the pretty girl in the pretty dress, with the ridiculously expensive shoes and eat food that a very nice family, in a beautiful home with creepy soothsayer painted rooms, had cooked for me and my best friend.

I took a deep breath, inhaling a sweet-smelling incense, burning away on the windowsill. I pulled at a red drape to reveal one of the Georgian windows. Through it, I could see the sun had set below the distant hills, and a forest surrounded us. The sky glowed a deep shade of pink and fairy lights seemed to make the gardens below sparkle. It had been quite a day.

There was a knock on the door.

I answered to a very handsome looking James. He had showered, and his hair still seemed damp, but I could smell a rose scented body wash emanating off of him and a slight hint of spiced vanilla aftershave. They had dressed him as wonderfully as they had dressed me. He wore a perfectly fitted blazer over a crisp white shirt, with trousers and, what looked like freshly shined dress shoes. He wore no tie, though I suspected they had provided him with one. He, instead, wore the collar open at the top button.

I was surprised he didn't tell me to stop drooling, but then I realised he'd been staring at me in the same way. He was taking me in... the dress... my legs... my chest...

I punched him in the rib, reverting back to my ingrained, boisterous ways. He stepped back and ran a hand through his damp hair.

"I don't know what to say, Loz. You look gorgeous."

"Not bad yourself, Clarke."

He looked down at himself and shrugged. "This is all a bit –"

"Bizarre?"

"Yeah." He shook it off and held out his arm. "Let's do this," he said, before adding, "Almighty Saviour of the Universe."

When we'd cleared the staircase – at a snail pace thanks to my heels – we were greeted by a suited and booted Marcus. He looked incredibly smart and graceful, despite his large frame, in his white shirt and black velvet tie.

"Beautiful," he said, matter-of-factly.

"Thank you," answered James. I elbowed him in the side.

Marcus chuckled. "Shall we?"

He gestured for us to follow him under the stairs and towards the rear of the house. He opened one of the glossed doors and revealed a glass dining room. Candles hung from the ceiling on wooden plinths and below them was a long dining table.

To my utter and complete alarm, the table was already near full of people. James stepped closer to my side. Everyone had been chattering away, but upon our entry, had fallen silent. They all stared at me. I suddenly felt very clammy. Marcus put his hand on my arm, as though sensing my worry.

 I took in the people before me, scrutinising as they scrutinised me. They all had similar traits: Dark hair, olive skin and muscles. There were a few blondes, a fellow redhead, one or two greys, but those muscles… they were constant.

 "They're warriors," I stated.

 "They're my family," Marcus corrected. "All of us, one big family. We live together and train together. Please don't be overwhelmed. They're all very excited to meet you."

 The silence was overwhelming in its own right, so I was monumentally grateful when Debbie stood up from her seat at the opposite end of the table and walked up to us. The feeling of familiarity and comfort around Debbie was actually quite astonishing, given what we'd been through. When she held out her hand, I took it and let her lead me alongside the seated people and sit James and I together beside her.

The dining chair was soft on my back and I was grateful to it. It had been a very physically demanding day… not to mention mentally exhausting.

The moment we pulled in our chairs the pleasant, eager chatter resumed along the table. I took in the food laid out before us. No monkey heads. James elbowed me gently in the arm and nodded his head towards the turkey in the centre of the table and the surrounding bowls. There were curries, naan breads and onion bhajis. There were beansprouts, spring rolls, sweet and sour chicken, black bean sauce over vegetables and a large bowl of rice. Then there was a wide selection of pizzas and fries, jacket potatoes with various fillings. My stomach garbled loudly, and James sniggered.

"Who cooked all of this?" I asked, leaning to Debbie.

She nodded her head towards her father. "We did."

"You? All of you?" I asked, astonished.

She nodded enthusiastically. "You came on a good night. Once a month, we all come together and cook one dish each. It's basically potluck night. There's always something you'll like."

"So, it's not usually like this, every night?"

Debbie laughed to herself and looked around at her family. "We usually dress in jeans and t-shirts. The fancy dress is for you."

Debbie had changed as well. She was wearing a burgundy velvet dress that showed off the curve of her hips. The sleeves stopped just above her wrists. This was the first time I noticed she wore a wedding ring. She caught me looking.

"Shall I introduce you?" She turned to her husband. "I know you're trying to not seem too eager, but if you'd like to say hello, you're allowed."

He smiled down at his wife, revealing a perfectly white, straight set of teeth. He had dark blonde hair, spiked on top of his head and hazel green eyes that creased at the corners when he smiled.

"I'd quite like to say hello. Yes." He leaned further forward so he could see me and James. "I'm Nicholas." Nicholas had the hint of an accent that I couldn't quite place, but I thought he sounded Scandinavian. "It's an honour to meet you... I'm sorry my wife attacked you, but... actually, I'm quite honoured that *she* had the honour of... sacrificing you... You know, so you could be reborn by the grace of Selene and lead us all into the next age. I hope we can finally have a future for our children, free from violence." He was smiling all the while he was speaking.

Debbie cleared her throat uncomfortably. "That was weird Hun. That was a weird thing to say."

Nicholas nodded his head. "Can I try again?"

"Best had."

"Hi, I'm Nicholas. You both look lovely this evening."

"Better." Debbie patted his arm and Nicholas leaned over to grab a slice of pepperoni pizza. My stomach rumbled again.

Debbie took my plate and filled it with a variety of food, before doing the same for James and then herself. James started inhaling his food beside me and I bit hastily into a slice of pizza. The grease ran down my throat and the melted cheese was heavenly. I actually had to stop myself from moaning again and suddenly spared a brief thought for Marley and Richards. They'd have loved this spread. I wondered what was going on back at the station. I wondered if they felt a little less hostile after getting a good night's sleep. I shook off a random tingle of apprehension.

I leaned over to Debbie and Nicholas. "You said you have children?" Nicholas nodded. "Fourteen."

"Fourteen?" I shouted, prompting a few heads to turn. Debbie and Nicolas both laughed, from deep in their chests. I looked at James, who continued to eat.

"Fourteen what?" he asked with a mouth full of naan.

"Fourteen children, James."

"Woah."

"Right?"

Debbie picked a sweet potato fry from her husband's plate. "We're quite a lot older than we look, remember." I pondered this while I tried a spring roll. It was good.

James laughed.

"I have to say, if I could live that long, I think that's how I'd fill my time, too." Another elbow to the ribs. He rubbed his side, still laughing. "How old are they?"

"Our youngest will be six in May, "Nicholas said. "And our eldest is... two hundred and twelve."

"How did you meet?" James asked.

Debbie smiled at her husband. "He saved my life. I was in Sweden, following up on a lead. Reports of a group of Erebus controlled men praying on young women. I was only twenty at the time and I was eager to prove myself. It took me a month to make the journey, and when I finally found their hideout, they ambushed me. They'd seen me coming a mile away, had spies at the dock. Nicholas was the senior Warrior in the area at the time and he'd had his own people monitoring the situation when he heard a foreigner was coming to town. Good thing too. Him and his people had fought valiantly to protect me and together we ended them all."

"How romantic," James said, without much enthusiasm.

"It really was. He was so brave." She kissed her husband on the cheek and he nuzzled his forehead on hers. I cleared my throat, trying not to pay too much attention to the small space between my leg and James's.

"So," I pressed on, "is that what you think happened with Carl Taylor? Is that how he managed to blow his cell up? It's going to be fun explaining that one, if we ever find a way to go back and don't get arrested for kidnapping you and stealing a police vehicle."

Debbie turned to me with a very confused expression. "Carl Taylor?"

"Yeah, the guy from the station. Did you suspect he was being controlled by Erebus? It's definitely possible. He rose up the ranks pretty quickly and had his own bodyguards too, which is unheard of in a gang of that size."

"What are you talking about?" Debbie asked. She sounded panicked.

"Debbie, my dear," Marcus called over. "Carl Taylor, the boy you looked into before you left a week ago."

A few more people started to listen in, looking concerned. A grey-haired man with a reddish face and a girl of no more than sixteen.

I stepped in. "The explosion, remember? That's why we came and found you in the hospital. You'd broken into the station, took out a few officers and tried to get to Taylor. There was an explosion, you were injured, you tried to run, and two officers, our friends, Richards and

Marley, they caught you. They took you to the hospital unconscious."

Debbie stood up from the table, sending her chair flying backwards into the wall behind her. The room fell silent.

Nicholas stood up and put his hand on her arm. She held his other hand and looked up at him.

"I can't remember how I got to that hospital bed. When I woke up, there was a woman with me and…" She held a hand to her head. "She said something to me but can't remember what it was. The next thing I remember was Lauren standing over me. Even now. I'm trying to picture her face. I can't. I don't remember a man at all. Nor Carl Taylor."

Several people had now stood up and started leaving the room, returning with their coats. Marcus made his way around the table and spoke to the room. "This is unprecedented. The Erebus has never before been able to penetrate our minds and effect our memories. This is a strength we have never faced. Perhaps, when Selene resurrected Lauren, Erebus felt it. Or perhaps Erebus grew in power first and Selene decided it was time? We may, perhaps, never know. I suggest we call it a night. Can I please ask, the senior members of the household to meet me down the hall? Lauren, James, would you mind joining us?"

I didn't know what had just happened, but there was a pit in my stomach. James threw his jacket over my shoulders and helped me up from my seat. A group of people gathered around Marcus and he led us all out of the dining room and back out onto into the hallway.

"What's going on?" I whispered to Debbie.

She looked at her husband, then to me. "I had my memory taken. I can't remember a Carl Taylor. A man I'm supposed to have been researching for a week and surveying. If the last thing I remember is that female police officer, then *she* is the one who did this to me."

"*What?*" I asked. My face felt cold. "That's impossible. She's one of my best friends."

"The male too." She replied, seemingly not having heard my defiance.

"Richards? No! No, you're wrong." Then it dawned on me. "You're going to kill them."

"Lauren, we have to. Erebus has infiltrated your police force. And he's more powerful than ever."

Chapter Ten

As I tried to digest that, we walked around the corner and I nearly toppled over as three children ran past us. A little girl who was being chased stopped and turned to charge at the two little boys. I nearly choked when she flew through the air and kicked the tallest one in the face.

He took it really well, rubbing his jaw and *laughing,* as they took off running the other way. Debbie grabbed the little girl by the wrist and stopped her.

"Stop beating up your cousins," Debbie said. Then she started tickling the girl, who laughed uncontrollably. She let the girl go and stood up straight. I could see the resemblance. She had Debbie's brown eyes with the green flecks and Nicholas's dark blonde hair.

"The youngest?" I asked. Debbie stroked the girl's hair.

"This is Serenity."

"Lovely name."

"Thank you!" gushed the little girl.

She reminded me of me at that age. Fighting the world, standing up to boys, even down to the clunky boots…

My boots! That's where they went! She took off running after her cousins, my size sixes flopping and thudding as she struggled to pick up her feet.

"Leave the boots!" Nicholas called after her.

Serenity didn't stop running, but kicked her feet to either side. The boots flew off and she disappeared around the corner, her giggles echoing through the house. I scooped up my boots as we passed.

We entered a room far less appealing than the rest of the house. A single meeting table stood in the middle of four white walls and a projector hung from the ceiling. The atmosphere was heavy, and I was taken back to my Police Cadet classroom training as the sound of chair legs scrapping the floor echoed around the cold room.

I leaned against the far wall, watching everyone get comfortable. Debbie offered us a chair, but we both declined. I suppressed the urge to vomit.

Marcus stood up and everyone went quiet. "Ideas?" he asked.

There was a brief moment of silence, then an eruption of noise as everybody tried to speak at once. My ears were getting more sensitive by the hour and the noise made my head pulse. I closed my eyes and tried to focus on one person. Unsurprisingly, it was Debbie's and Nicholas's voices that stood out from the crowd.

"We should go now," I heard Debbie demand.

"We can't allow this infiltration to continue another minute," Nicholas shouted, slamming his fist on the table.

"Sheridan," I heard someone else say. "How can you say that? Holding off until we know more about the infiltration is only going to make the matter worse."

I opened my eyes and searched for Sheridan.

"I just think we need to take a step back and try to get an idea of the bigger picture," he said. He was a young man, though I really wasn't sure who was young in this room.

If his normal looking age was anything to go by, he can't have been more than twenty-five, and just as handsome as everybody else in this family. I wondered if it was a Warrior trait to be so beautiful or if it was just their bloodline and fitness regimes. He ran a hand across his stubbled chin with stress.

"Please! One person at a time!" Marcus boomed and the room fell silent. "Sheridan, I understand where you're coming from, I do, but I agree with your mother. The longer we leave it, the worse it'll get."

"Fine," Sheridan conceded. "But we need a full team. Let's not get blind-sided by rushing in without the numbers we need."

"Agreed," said Nicholas, smiling slightly at his son. Sheridan nodded, in a more serious way.

I suddenly felt like I wouldn't be able to suppress the urge to be sick for much longer. These people were discussing how best to go about killing my friends. To kill them and free them of the possession of something I haven't ever seen before – yet I was supposed to take everything they said at face value and allow them to slaughter people? I closed my eyes again, trying to block out the conversation. My skin burned and prickled and stung and it felt amazing and horrible all in one confusing minute, but it wasn't developing fast enough. A voice sung in my head, a high ringing of a voice, calm and clear.

Focus.

I jumped and my eyes flew open. The only person looking at me was James.

"Are you okay?"

I didn't know how to answer that. I closed my eyes again and did what must have been my own, exhausted, internal voice, told me to do. I focused.

Lead them.

That definitely wasn't my voice.

Make them listen. Show them who you are.

I don't know who I am.

Yes, you do.

I really didn't but the voice seemed so sure, I started to wonder. If everything we'd heard today was the truth, and honestly, it was getting exhausting trying to pretend that it wasn't, then Selene ran through my veins.

"Hello," I gasped. Debbie turned slightly in her seat, side-eying me.

You are me. We're the same. Body and soul, we are one. You need to let us both in to become who you truly were meant to be. Who you truly are.

A tear ran down my cheek. I don't know where I came from. I have no idea who I am.

Stop fighting us and all will become clear. Have faith.

Another tear. Debbie was facing me entirely and James had held my arm. I could feel an incredible rush of ice run through my body from my navel, up my stomach, through my chest, my throat, my mind.

I let it erupt. A wave burst from my body and the table in the centre of the room cracked. A loud, deafening noise as the wood split straight down the middle. All eyes fell on me. I gasped as the air I'd just expelled came rushing back into my lungs and I shook slightly at the sheer energy I had lost.

"I can hear her," I whispered to James.

"Who?" He looked to Debbie, whose eyes never left mine.

"Selene," I breathed. I tapped my temple. "Here. I can hear her." I felt empowered with confidence. I walked to the head of the table and stroked where the wood had cracked. I slid James's jacket off my shoulders, before handing it out to him. It was a ploy, to make him walk to me where I stood. As he did, and as he took hold of the jacket, I refused to let go for a second, staring into his eyes and hoping he understood that I wanted him to stay by my side. He did. This was how I wanted it, how I needed it. I needed him there. I wanted this family to understand that if they wanted me to lead them and they wanted me to leave my life behind, then I would keep the only person who actually knew me, by my side, the whole time.

I turned back to my audience. "These officers are my people. They're just as much my family as you are to each other."

Sheridan took the hand of a woman with the most beautiful red hair I had ever seen. It reminded me of a proud father, watching his child graduate. I found inspiration in that.

"I don't know where I came from. I don't know if I will ever know. I was a baby left on the side of the road, no mother, no father, no family at all. Until I met James." I reached out and held his hand. "Many years later – though perhaps not that many to you guys..." This earned laughter. "And I became a police officer. As the prophecy says, 'A warrior in her own right. A guardian of the people.' The officers you speak of are like me. They really are warriors. I've laughed with them, fought with them, had my life saved by them on more than one occasion, and vice versa."

I took a deep breath, before I said what I had to say.

"I don't know if what I've learned is true… that some of these people may as well already be dead. If this is the case, if being possessed by even a small part of Erebus means they are truly lost, and they have to die, then I say we move right now. This very second. I won't commit murder for you in blind faith. Acts such as that are what's wrong with the world. As humbled as I am by your generosity this evening – I will not take you at your word. I'm going to need proof. Show me proof, beyond a shadow of a doubt that Erebus is real. Show me beyond a shadow of a doubt, that my friends are already dead...and I'll help you...I'll lead you. If that's what you want."

James grabbed my arm and murmured in my ear, "We can't kill them, Loz. This whole thing is ridiculous." I turned to face him. "That's why you're coming." I whispered as quietly as I could, though I still believed they could all hear me. "I trust them. I do. I don't know why but I have this feeling in my gut that's telling me Richards and Marley need to die. James, I'm afraid that I could do it. I need you with me. Be my human guide." He shook his head.

"Loz, please. I don't have the same mind you do, right now. I'm out of place here. All I'm seeing is a bunch of religious fanatics trying to justify the murder of our best friends." There was a silence that hung heavy in the room. He hadn't tried to conceal his voice.

"I understand your hesitation." Marcus stood in the corner of the room. "I believe there's something I can say that might make it a little easier to trust that what we say is true."

"I doubt it." James grunted.

"It was the Spring of nineteen-ninety-five," Marcus began. "There had been a large spread of Erebus led attacks in a small town called Heywood." I felt James stiffen at the name of the town in which he'd been born. "Women were being targeted in the most grotesque way you could imagine. My wife and I were patrolling the streets one night, I think it was April twentieth, if memory serves." James inhaled sharply and an instant bead of sweat formed on his brow. "We heard a scream down an alley way. When we arrived, there was a woman with dark brown hair lying on the floor and a man standing over her, carrying a bundled baby."

Marcus slowly made his way across the room as he spoke. "The man was a nobody, a homeless drug user. You see, Erebus is drawn to chaos. It cannot thrive in a host unless there is already an element of darkness. This man had an abundance of it and Erebus had taken his body as his own and he used it as a weapon to murder the most beautiful thing this world has to offer. Mothers. He would take the baby, who knows where. We suspected he would use them as hosts so they could be raised back into society and wreak havoc."

Marcus now stood before James and I thought he would burst into tears at any moment.

"The woman was already dead. We couldn't save her. But you had best *believe* we saved that baby and avenged his mother's death. We made sure this version of Erebus could never orphan another child or widow another husband again. I remember the woman's name like she was one of my own daughters. Maria Clarke. Mother of one son, wife of Lawrence." There was a heavy silence and I could hear James's breathing, short and erratic.
"How could you know about her?" James whispered, holding back tears.

"My wife and I posed as police officers. As the guardians of the people and we returned the baby to his father. I had never seen a man look so helpless and broken before. I believe he began his training the day after he buried his wife. Today he has a skill set to rival even the most experienced Warrior. A skill he passed onto his son and then, one day, a little girl who, who would know it, would become the saviour of us all."

He looked at me, then back to James. "We're not just shadows in the night, fighting something that doesn't concern you. We remember every victim, every host, every kill and we make damned sure the people left behind are thriving in their lives. We're more than just killers. Certainly more than religious fanatics. We're people too, James. We can't free a host from the possession of Erebus, but we can kill the two as one and it's an evil, yes, but it is a necessary evil to stop worse things from happening to good, kind people. We do what we do, what needs to be done, so that what happened to your mother, never happens again.

"Now, James, are you with us?"

James remained silent. Marcus took my hand and wrapped his arm around James shoulders, resting his forehead on his. "Are you with her?" There wasn't even a flow of air between the question being asked and the answer it received. "I'm always with her." Tears streamed from his eyes. Marcus squeezed my hand tightly before placing it in James's and taking a step back. "I never forgot you, boy. You were the only one we could save. Selene works in mysterious ways, but I believe it is no coincidence you're here tonight."

I leaned into James and looked up at him. He wiped his face on the back of his hand and sniffed, before looking down at me. "You good?" I asked.

"I never even told you that. I told nobody that she'd been murdered. Not a soul. It's the very reason I became a police officer." I leaned my face on his arm, squishing my nose into his shirt, and nodded against him. "I knew.

Your Dad told me. I just knew if you wanted to talk about it you would have. So, I never let on that I knew...it's the reason I became an officer, too." A sob escaped his lips and he kissed my forehead and we turned, with no shame, to the room again. "I won't kill them, James. I just need to see if it's true, with my own eyes." James nodded down at me. He agreed.

"We go tonight," I demanded of the people I had just that night met. They all moved as one under my command.

There was another debate about who would attend. It was decided that James and I had to show our face to gain entry and raise the least suspicion. However, because I didn't have the instinct to sense Erebus yet, and neither would James, it became concerningly clear that Debbie would have to come with us. We couldn't very well just waltz back into the station having had our own colleagues hunting us down for stealing a car and releasing a prisoner.

We came up with a story to cover ourselves, not so far out of the realms of possibility that it wouldn't be believed, but still clutching at straws. Apparently, when we took over from Marley and Richards, Jane Doe (Debbie) had pretended that she needed the toilet and when I had tried to assist her, she had attacked me and

James, all of which would be corroborated by our witnesses, the nurses. Then it gets a little sticky and we weren't sure if they'd buy it, but we would say that Jane Doe (Debbie) had managed to conceal a gun and pulled it on us, threatening that if we didn't do exactly as she asked, she'd shoot us and the nursing staff. So, we complied.

Essentially the idea was that we were the victims and after we'd played along to keep ourselves alive, we found an opportunity to jump her, take the gun and arrest her, eventually making our way back to the station to let everyone know what had gone down.

There were many holes. However, as soon as Debbie was in a cell, she'd be able to make her judgements through an earpiece and advise a team on the outside who was who. Or, who was under the possession of Erebus and who wasn't. They were presuming Richards and Marley weren't the only two. Then one by one, the Warriors would infiltrate the station undercover as officers (apparently these guys could pose as the Pope if they wanted to) some would be in a cell over night for disorderly conduct.

And then there was us. James and me. We were told, in no uncertain terms, to stay out of the way. To observe as training. They may have known more than me about my purpose in life, amongst many other things, but they unfortunately didn't know much else. We had no intention of sitting idly by...I saw no scenario where I could allow my friends to be killed.

There was an interesting moment as we packed a hold-all of ammunition into a box, ready for the helicopter we were waiting on. The ammunition in question was a large selection of what I now know the Warriors call Stilétos, as it had been a Greek Warrior who had created the design and spread the word on how to create a dagger from the moon rock. I quite liked that actually, though the daggers still made my stomach turn slightly. A feeling I thought was perfectly understandable under the circumstances.

Debbie was making sure they were boxed up properly when she'd asked, "How long have you and James been together?"

I snorted.

"We're not together. Not like that."

Debbie waved me off. "No, I know the story, I heard my father. I knew none of that, by the way. I don't want you thinking I had all these secrets about James and his family, I really didn't know."

I smiled. "I didn't think that."

"Good, I'm glad. I know I get a little over excited about who you are, but you have to understand… I'm really old, Lauren. I've been around longer than anybody would really want to be and I've seen a lot of darkness in my years. I don't know, being raised on those prophecies – they were the bedtime stories for us – and finally… we can taste the end, you know? It's really a huge deal for us and I hope that one day, you'll see it as a great thing. I hope, for you and for James, that you'll find a way to figure out that you're more than friends, you're more than family even. The way he looks at you, the way he's so calm around all of this.

"Think about it. How insane this must all seem to you, but you have an edge, you have the benefits of these newfound instincts and power to go with this explanation. You can believe it and you can run with everything going on right now, because inside you, you know that this is real. You just know. For him, though…" She shook her head. "He must be freaking out right now… like I said, I've been around for centuries, I know love when I see it."

I thought about that. Everyone knew James loved me. "I know he loves me. I love him. He just, can't seem to see past this friendship long enough to notice that I'm head over heels in love with him. But he's everything I have, and I can't be the one to risk losing that." I looked back towards the house in the dark of the night. There were crickets ticking away and the grass around us. It was a really beautiful night. Debbie finished up and we both heard the blades of the helicopter chopping away in the distance. At the same time, we saw the two of their lights, flashing brighter as they got closer.

The door opened from the house and the team filed out. I smiled internally as I saw James. We'd been given a further change of clothes. A police uniform, but not the ones we had on earlier. A few other members of the family wore the same thing, while someone else was dressed in their formalwear – the drunk and disorderly, I'd thought.

Debbie whispered to me, before James was in earshot, "Take it from someone who's been in love with the same man for over three-hundred years. Every day without the one you love, knowing how much you love them, is a day carelessly mistreated."

James came over and Debbie gave us some space.

"Are you ready for this?" he asked.

I thought about it. Maybe now was the time. Not another second to waste. Now or never. Except it's always easier to tell yourself you'll do something than it is to actually do it. So, instead, I just kissed him on the cheek and said, "I'm always ready." You liar.

Chapter Eleven

I had always imagined that being in a helicopter would be really cool. I was wrong.

It was deafeningly loud, and we had to wear large headphones just to hear each other speak. Nicholas had explained that it sounded so much worse for us because of our sensitive hearing. Every time I had to adapt to my new enhancements, I found myself wondering why I'd never had them before. If what Debbie had said was anything to go by, and let's face it, it probably was, then I was born a Warrior. Why were all these strengths and abilities only just now manifesting? Where was the line between what a typical Warrior is capable of and what *I* am capable of because of Selene?

Speaking of, the voice hadn't spoken to me since the meeting room. I'd tried talking to her. I'd tried asking her all these questions and despite everyone around me, I suddenly felt quite alone.

I took in my company. James sat next to me, tapping his foot nervously. Debbie sat to the right of me and Nicholas sat across from her. A short woman with cropped dark hair and an arrow tattoo on her wrist sat across from me and then next to her was a young-looking girl, possibly around nineteen, possibly around seventy. It really was a guessing game. I heard Nicholas call her Lois. Was she their daughter? Granddaughter? Who knew? Marcus, Sheldon and the four other members of the Sina family had taken their place on the second helicopter. The atmosphere was serious but there were a few things I wanted to get straightened out.

"The way I can… the way I... You know?"

"What?" Debbie leant forward so she could see my face.

"The table thing."

"That's just you. It's a lot, isn't it?" I nodded. "Okay. The average Warrior has heightened speed, strength, sense of smell, sight, hearing and taste. Our instincts are beyond the average humans. We're actually quite on par with dogs and other animals. It's not actually out of the realms of possibility that animals are also descended from Gaia."

"Perhaps that's a little off the mark, my love." Nicholas smiled at me. He'd seen my confusion growing as Debbie went off on one of her information dump tangents.

"Right," she corrected herself. "Everything we have comes from ourselves. Our abilities are evolutionary benefits that we've inherited from Gaia. Humans are evolved from the life of Eden. They're a pure species. A simple species, James. No offence." James waved her off. "Selene was a whole separate entity. The gifts that you have come from her. You draw power from outside forces. You'll be able to manipulate things like light, vibrations, maybe even gravitational pull."

"Like the elements? Like…fire?" She shook her head.

"The elements are something entirely different. They can't be controlled. Witches in the human world believe that they can draw strength from the elements. That much would be true for you, but to control them, to manipulate them. That's something beyond even this world. But there are people in our world who can show you how to use elemental inspiration, such as drawing strength from a fire or energy from the Earth. It's complicated but Nicholas is actually very good at it."

I looked sideways at James and I could tell he had the same thought as me. A memory. Back in Tony Marques's gym, where I created flames from nothing. From just my hands.

I wondered if now was a good time to bring it up, but I saw something flash in James's eyes that seemed to shut down my thought process. I'd leave it for now.

Instead, I smiled at Nicholas and said, "Sure. That sounds great." He seemed thrilled that I'd accepted his help.

"Of course, it's mostly a placebo effect for me," he explained "A way to visualise strength. But for you… I'm excited to see the effect."

"I look forward to it."

The rest of the journey went by quickly and we were soon touching down on an open field.

I hopped down from the chopper with more difficulty than I cared to admit. It'd been a long day and my legs were tired. That was my excuse as I tumbled to my knees. James laughed and I gave him a dead arm.

I looked around and tried to pinpoint exactly where we'd landed. The station did have a lot of surrounding farmlands, but I couldn't see the lights of any shops or streets in the immediate vicinity.

I cracked my back and stretched my arms out above my head. James seemed as confused by our location as I was. The second helicopter had arrived before we did, and the two groups of the same family convened together to discuss some things. I didn't want to miss out on any vital information, but I also didn't want to get in the way.

James took out his phone. I'd left mine at the house. He pulled up a map and raised an eyebrow.

"We're in Greensway Park," he said, confused.

"But that's got to be, what, three miles away?"

"We had to fly here to save time," said Marcus, having overheard us, "but we don't want to tip them off. Two helicopters are, unfortunately, not discreet. We'll drive from here."

I hadn't acknowledged the three Jeeps parked up in the distance. I suspected James couldn't even see them now. Another perk. There were a few more kinks to work out, but as soon as Marcus patted Debbie on the shoulder and Debbie came over to us, I knew we were ready to go. She handed out two Stilétos. We took them a little gingerly, prompting her to chuckle.

"We're not expecting you to fight. We just don't want you to be defenceless."

I winked at her. "With these fists, we're never defenceless." This earned me an eye roll.

We started the walk towards the jeeps, tucking the Stilétos into our jeans pockets.

I knew we had arrived when the blue police sign lit up the car.

Lois was sitting next to me at the time and as we'd pulled into the car park, she started getting twitchy. I couldn't tell if this was a good thing or not. Getting herself worked up for the fight I thought.

She was dressed in black combats and t-shirt with a utility belt around her waist. She would be one of the backup fighters if things turned south. Looking at the definition of her biceps as she stretched, I was grateful to have her there.

We drove up to the far end of the car park and stopped beside a row of small trees.

"Okay, are we ready?" Debbie asked as Nicholas pulled out a set of handcuffs and swung them around on her index finger.

"Ready," James said with more conviction that I think he felt.

Debbie stood in front of him and planted her feet in a stance I recognized well.

As did James. "What are you doing?"

"I'm really sorry," she said, and punched him square in the nose. James leaned back and held his face as he cried out in pain.

"What the hell!" I exclaimed.

I pulled his hands from his face so I could look. Blood ran over his lips.

"It's not broken," Debbie assured us. When she walked up to me, I held up my finger. "You are not punching *me* in the face."

"No, you're punching *me*. And make it good. We heal fast and we need it to look real. Scuffs on your knuckles, bruises on my face. Let's do it." She shuffled and cracked her neck in preparation.

"I'm not going to punch you in the face."

"I'll do it," James offered, raising his fists while the blood poured from his nose.

Nicholas stepped beside me. "You know how to throw a punch?"

"Of course, I do."

"Yeah, I know you can. You had no problem in the hospital." She made a fair point.

"Yes, but I didn't know then what I know now. I kind of like you now and I kind of wanted to kill you then."

"That's really sweet, Lauren. But we're on the clock, my love, so just wallop me before I make Nicholas do it, and he really hates to do it."

"I do. It's not good. We did this once in Moscow, in the seventies. She had to play the victim, I had to play the villain, it wasn't good at all. I cried for days."

Debbie nodded in agreement. "Come on. I can take it. Show me what you've got."

I exhaled and assumed a boxing stance. I pulled back and swung from my hips, jabbing out at her nose. I heard a crunch upon impact which I tried not to think about as I swung again and punched her in the side of her eye. I tensed and took a step forward so I wouldn't stumble.

Marcus leaned against the side of the Jeep and laughed.

"Beautiful." He clapped his large hands together. "We should go now."

Debbie held out her hands and Nicholas fastened the cuffs on her. "Can you get out of those?"

She nodded, her nose crooked and bleeding, and a large bruise forming on the right side of her face.

Nicholas lifted her chin. "You're amazing. I love you." He kissed her cheek so he wouldn't hurt her broken nose. A knot of guilt twisted in my stomach, but I knew she would heal, and I knew this was for the greater good.

I thought of my colleagues in there. My friends. I tried to separate myself from the image of what needed to be done if everything they'd said proved to be true and I prayed that I wouldn't have to be the one to do it. I looked at my knuckles. They were only a little red. James saw.

"Years of glove free boxing and now you've got accelerated healing. It's going to take more than that to scuff up those fists."

I lifted my hand to his face. He didn't move. "Your nose okay?"

"All good. You ready?"

"Almost," I said, before punching my fist, as hard as I could, into the ground. The crack I caused in the tarmac prompted a whistle from Marcus and Sheridan, who had been throwing on a hi-vis police jacket. I looked down at my fists. There was a streak of blood where the skin had torn away. I could literally feel the tissue already trying to heal. Pulling together. Debbie walked up to James and nodded her head, sharply. "Don't be gentle."

"I won't be," he said as he grabbed her by the shoulder and steered her towards the station lights. I followed by her side.

A thousand thoughts raced through my head as we approached the doors. I was worried about them not believing us. I was terrified that more people had been taken over. I was confused at how this had happened, at how so much energy had congregated in one area. I didn't understand if Erebus had moved from one person to another of if my people were being taken to another location for the possession. Most importantly, I was worried for James. He was so ready for this, so sure that he wanted to help me and to help them. It was easy to understand why.

I'd known his mother had been murdered and I'd known when. All these years I had been fully aware that his father had taken to his training because he had felt useless in the darkest moment of his life. He had turned his grief into something powerful. Who could have ever imagined these worlds would collide in this way? The coincidences seemed so strong. He must have thought the same thing. I pondered the idea that there were no coincidences. This world has always been a part of ours. How many murders had I heard on the news? How many attacks, fires, thefts, gangs taking control of towns? How many were humans being humans and how many were under the influence of Erebus? It made me question what I'd thought of humanity. It made me question a lot of things. I was conflicted. A basic instinct steered my brain to accepting all of this as fact. Erebus was real. It had possessed my friends and now my friends had to die. Terrifyingly, the part of me that felt this, was dominant to the part of me who could never imagine this was real. Who would rather die than hurt them.

 I could hear my heartbeat in my head. Erratic, fast, strong. I could hear James's too. Just the same as mine. He was nervous but he was controlling it.

There was always a familiar smell, walking into the station. The smell of burned coffee beans and leather. I tried to take solace in my surroundings. I tried to stop thinking of this situation as alien. This was my home five, sometimes six or seven days of the week. This was my battlefield. I tried to remember that and gather strength from the familiar floor, with each step, imagining it gave me power. These floors were my stage. Mine and James's. This is the place where we knew who we were. Police Officers. The good guys. No blurred lines. No Selene. No Gaia. No prophesized Theia. I wasn't the saviour. I was PC Smith and he was PC Clarke.

 We made our way to the front desk. The receptionist looked up and I knew, just by that immediate reaction, that she was surprised to see us. Before we even reached her, she had picked up the phone. I wondered who she was calling. I tried to listen in, but she'd hung up before I'd locked onto her voice. Maybe Debbie knew.

"Becca."

James smiled down at her, keeping a firm hold on Debbie's shoulder.

"Could you do us a favour and call DCI Rowlands down here for us. We've had quite a day and I believe he'll be wanting to know what's been going on." I could hear the truth in his voice. We really had had one hell of a day.

"Where the bloody hell have you been?"

The three of us turned in unison to see DCI Rowlands marching over from an office across the way. He took in the scene before him and came to a halt a few feet away. I saw Debbie's eyes narrow. She was trying to figure out who was possessed and who wasn't. When I saw her relax, I let out a breath I didn't realise I'd been holding. DCI Rowlands was safe.

"Okay then," he said, taking in our injuries and then resting his eyes on Debbie. "You." Debbie scowled. "Her, you can put in a cell and then I would like a very long chat with the both of you."

I tried to resist the urge to smile. This was going to plan. We would take Debbie to her cell where she would swiftly make her escape and then while James and I were

145

explaining our version of events, the rest of the team would be doing a reconnaissance of the building and figure out who, if anyone, was under the influence. Simple.

"Obviously, I can't allow you to take her anywhere alone."

Or not so simple...

DCI Rowlands waved someone over from behind us and I knew it wasn't a good sign when I saw Debbie, subtly slip a hand from her cuffs and her whole-body tense at the ready. James saw it too and my heart clenched as I saw him reach under his jacket and wrap his hand around what I knew to be his concealed dagger. Would he try to kill Debbie if she tried to hurt Richards or Marley?

I turned my head to see, to my shock, Carl Taylor, in full police uniform, swaggering over to our group and come to a halt by DCI Rowlands's side.

"What can I do for you?" he asked me. I felt it then. That famous instinct everyone had been speaking about. I felt like someone had poured oil over my skin and all my senses stood on edge in preparation for the perceived threat. It was incredibly overwhelming, but I was grateful to have felt it. Now I would know. Because Carl Taylor was, without a doubt, under the possession of Erebus. And now I remembered that familiar feeling. It's similar to what I had felt when Richards and Marley had touched me...so...it was true?

I hadn't even a second to gather my thoughts. I'd assumed we would go along with it until we were in a more private setting. Apparently not. Debbie pulled her other hand from the cuffs and reached into her boot for her Stiléto. Without thinking, I pulled James out of the way. Debbie lunged forward, blade pointing straight for Carl. With a sudden wave of his hand, he deflected her and she flew in a spiral across the room.

She crashed into the coffee machine and landed like a ragdoll in a heap on the floor. My mind reeled. Was this evidence enough?

DCI Rowlands turned purple. "What on Earth – "he began, though he didn't get to finish as the next back hand was for him, and he flew a lot further. Rowlands went straight into the wall, with a twist and a crack. I just knew as I took in his slumped and creased figure that his neck was broken. I gasped and tried to shove James behind me. Surely, that was enough to convince him and me, that this was real.

I could hear the receptionist's heels clicking as she ran across the floor and out of the doors. At least someone got out safe. Or so I thought. My world came crashing down with the events that followed. Richards burst through the door, holding Becca by her neck. "Richards!"

I yelled. I could see it now. His eyes were darker. His skin mottled. "Richard?" I asked, hoping I could break through. "Let her go. Please." Richards tilted his head and with a brief snap of his wrist, broke Becca's neck. I gasped as her body slackened in his hold and he tossed her to the side like a discarded wrapper. Carl turned and smiled.

"Finally. I've been waiting for you. We need to have a little chat."

Chapter Twelve

I could feel the cool hilt of the dagger between my belt and my shirt. I wondered how fast I could draw it. There could be no doubt. That wasn't Richards anymore. I compared his face with Carls. Carl seemed to look the same as he did on the bust, but Richards looked...he looked like a decaying corpse. Even if there was some way to get rid of whatever had possessed him, it seemed his body was already dead. My heart broke. This wasn't happening. I looked at James and could see that he'd noticed this too. His mouth was set in a hard line. "Oh Richards." I murmured sadly. At least we wouldn't have to worry about killing him. Erebus got there first. A wave of anger rippled through me and I nearly threw myself at Carl, until twenty or so officers surrounded us.

I allowed myself a brief moment to believe these people were here to help us, until the sickening feeling swept over me and I realised, in horror, that they were all possessed. All of them. I noted an elderly man near the exit who had given me my entry interview and was days from retirement. A young boy who was part of the new recruits we'd seen that morning. In fact, a few of them were. All of these people couldn't be saved? I refused to accept it. They all had the same dead man walking look. Dark under eyes. Mottled pale skin. It was like the possession was trying to burst out of them and their skin cracked, peeled and gave way under the force.

Then I saw her.

Marley.

Tiny in her frame. Her eyes unrecognizable. She looked worse than the rest. I looked around, between them and Carl and suddenly I realised. "Erebus needs chaos." I said to nobody in particular. "Carl can take it because he's evil at his core...but my friends, the officers here...they're good."

"He won't be able to sustain these bodies for very long." Debbie grunted, confirming my fears. Their bodies were decaying. They were already dead – or close to it. Now I understood. The humans evil enough to sustain Erebus were lost to humanity anyway and the humans who were too good to survive needed to be put out of their misery. I looked into Marley's eyes. They were vacant. She was just a vessel now. A tear ran down my cheek. She didn't deserve this. I nearly cracked right there and then, until I found a way to replace my grief with anger. I looked to Becca, dead on the foyer floor. Dead at the hands of Richards – poor Richards. Erebus had killed my friends. It wasn't them we would be killing. It was *it*. The parasite. The decaying officers started closing in. James and I put our backs together so we couldn't be attacked from behind. Carl took a few steps towards us. I thought back to the stupid boy I had tackled and pinned against a wall. Had he been under the influence then? Why had he allowed me to do such a thing?

"You've messed up quite a few things for me," he said, still walking towards us slowly. "I have to say, I'm not your biggest fan."

"Yeah, well I'm not exactly a huge fan of yours either," I sneered, trying to hide the fear in my voice. He threw his head back and laughed. The sound filled the foyer.

"Where is everyone?" I asked, a little more confidently.

He stopped laughing. "Out. I sent them out." He tapped his temple. "Funny little things, humans, aren't they? Small minded. Not very intelligent. Always waiting for someone else to save them." He bit his lip and cocked his head to the side, taking me in as he reached a hand out and started stroking Marley's hair. I wanted to rip his arm off. He continued. "Not you…no. There's something. Something unusual in you. A familiarity."

Carl dropped his hand from Marley's hair and flew into my face, blowing a strand of hair away. His breath smelt like iron. "Hmm." He stared into my eyes and I had a sickening feeling, as though he could see inside my mind. I felt exposed but I refused to let him see that he scared me. I stared back. I stared into his mind. There was nothing.

I had never known Carl Taylor. Only the basics. Only child, grew up in the foster system. I could empathise. He'd turned to petty theft at the age of twelve, full-fledged criminal by the age of eighteen. Then he met Mr. Lorde and got himself involved in the heavy stuff. Dealing class-A drugs to anyone who could afford it. Answering to a man who we were sure lead a gang, spread out across three continents.

"Oh," I breathed.

That's when it dawned on me. I realised how I'd messed things up for him. "You never wanted Carl Taylor. You wanted Mr. Lorde."

"Francis Bateman, actually. That's his real name. I have put a lot of work into finding out everything I could about him. Brilliant man. Smarter than most. Powerful. Made you lot think he had more above him that he did. He was at the forefront of more schemes and more destruction that you had ever uncovered. You hadn't even begun to scratch the surface of what Francis Bateman was responsible for. Drug rings, human trafficking, black market organ harvesting, dealing weapons to terrorists. Ooh, the chaos that man wreaked."

He stepped back shaking his head in an exasperated sort of way. He suddenly turned, pointing his finger at me. James reached for my hand. I had almost forgotten he was there and was grateful for the warmth of his skin. I grasped his hand in return, our sweat making the grip slip.

"And then *you. Blew. His. Hand. Off?*"

My stomach clenched.

"And got him arrested. Now, that wouldn't have been much of a problem. I'd intended on taking *you* when you had me pinned against that wall. Planned on using your body in any way I wanted. No problem. Infiltrate the local police force, find out where they took Bateman, then hunt him down, take his body and break free. Simple." He licked his lips. "It should have been simple. I should have seen you lot coming." He ran a hand through his hair. "I should've known. I don't know how you hid your Warrior stench from me, I had no idea who you were until you threw that man clean across the yard. By then I'd changed my mind. You'd... you had inspired me. Why not follow in the footsteps of great Warriors? Hmm? Undercover as a police officer. Imagine the fun I could have with that."

I reached my hand behind my back and wrapped it around the hilt of the Stiléto. I could feel energy buzzing through my body.

"And I did. I expanded." He opened his arms, gesturing to the surrounding officers. "Small minds. Easy to manipulate. Easy to make believe I'd worked here for years. No one dared question me and one by one I implanted myself into these bodies. Only took a couple of hours. Ha. It's been great fun, I have to say." He nodded, enthusiastically. "And then I waited for you. Waited for you to come back for me."

"How did you make me forget you?" Debbie's voice made me jump as it rang out from across the room. She had come to and was pulling herself up from the floor.

Carl rolled his eyes at her. "Because, you stupid little girl, I'm stronger than you."

Debbie was on her feet now. She'd picked the dagger up from the floor and held it tightly in her hand. She was outside the circle of surrounding officers.

"Erebus has never been able to do that," she coughed and held her ribs.

I wondered just how injured she was and how long it would take her to heal. Her nose already looked perfect and unbroken, so I'd guessed another five minutes depending on the damage.

"I *am* Erebus!" Carl yelled. "I am more powerful now than I have ever been. Your days are numbered. One by one I come back to myself and when I find a vessel strong enough to hold all of my scattered parts, I'll make away with all of you. This filthy planet and its filthy species." He snapped his head to me again. "But first, I'll make you pay for your insubordination."

I snarled. "I don't answer to you." It was now or never. "You killed my friends." I pulled out the Stiléto and lunged for him. Seeing me coming, he grabbed the wrist that held the dagger with one hand, and with the other, he lifted me into the air by my throat. I could feel his fingers crushing into my windpipe and I tried gasping for a breath that wouldn't come. There was a blur in the corner of my eye and Carl screamed in pain, before dropping me to the floor.

I looked up and saw James had plunged his dagger into Carls side. He'd tried to pull it out, but Carl gripped him by the hair and flung him over the heads of the circle of officers.

"James!" I screamed.

At that same moment, I heard a loud smash from above and looked up to see the skylight raining down on us. A small grenade followed, clinking as it bounced across the tiled floor. My eyes widened and I started to run. Before I could, the grenade exploded, but not in the way I had imagined. Gas started to pour out and sent a fog swirling around us. Shouts followed. My vision was impaired. I could only hear grunts and screams.

I tried to crawl across the floor and found that the circle had dispersed. Booted feet stood on my fingers. I coughed through the mist.

"James!" I called.

I hadn't seen where he'd landed and envisioned him lying with a broken neck like Rowlands and Becca. I shook the thought away.

"James!" I tried again.

Someone grabbed me by the scruff of the neck and pulled me up off the floor. I swung, trying to punch and kick.

"Stop! Lauren! Come now, my girl."

I could hear the familiar sound of Marcus and I nearly collapsed as I felt his strong arms pull me into him.

"You're alright. Don't fight. Come with me."

I let him half-lead, half-drag me until I felt my arm lean into a wall. He pulled me down, so we were crouched low.

"Listen to me. You *can* see. Your eyesight is a Warrior's eyesight. You have to focus." He sounded like the voice of Selene in my head and I wished she was here again. I wished for that comfort. I felt so alone here.

"I can't."

He grabbed my face. "You can."

I thought of James out there amongst the smoke and forced myself to focus. I felt Marcus wrap something around my mouth – a scarf, I thought – so I could breathe. I took a deep breath, closed my eyes and counted backwards from ten.

When I hit zero, I opened my eyes again. I could see. It was almost like infrared. Everything seemed to take on a neon hue. I found Marcus's face and could tell by the crease of his eyes above his mask, that he was smiling.

"Well done." He patted my shoulder. "You dropped this."

He handed me my Stiléto and I gripped it gratefully.

"I lost James."

I looked at him, pleadingly. He looked around at the chaos. I saw what he saw. The Sinas, the Prices and all the others, the team made of his family, in an affray. Hi-vis met black as the Erebus fought the Warriors.

Marcus gripped my jacket. "You fight to kill, or you die." This was the soldier. He had no time for anything but the fight. He was right. I nodded my head and stood up. Marcus ran into the smoke. I flinched when I saw him plunge a dagger into the chest of the boy who had started his job not twenty-four hours ago.

No. I told myself. Erebus. He killed Erebus. The chaos feasting parasite who just murdered DCI Rowlands and threw James across the room. I resolved myself and ran forwards. Something barged into me from my left and I skidded across the floor, landing on my backside. I stared into the open eyes of a member of the Sina family. A man I recognized from the dinner table. His neck twisted at an unusual angle. This way of killing seemed to be a trend for this thing. I tore my eyes away from the fallen Warrior and turned to see a shadow fly at me. I lifted the dagger just quickly enough as a man jumped on me, wrapping his hands around my throat. I plunged the Stiléto up and felt as it pushed through his shirt... his flesh... his sternum... and up into his heart.

I saw him gasp. I swallowed the part of me that felt like I was the bad guy. One twist of the dagger and the light left his already lifeless eyes.

His body fell limp on mine and I toyed with the idea of just lying there. His blood running from the blade onto me. Urgh.

I shoved the body off me. When I looked at him, there was a black liquid oozing from his nose, his eyes, his mouth and his ears.

I jumped as I felt arms around my shoulders. I tilted my head and saw it was Debbie. I exhaled in relief.

"It's the decay of Erebus," she shouted into my ear. She noticed the body beside me and whimpered. "Lewis." She breathed. "He was my Great Uncle." In the distance, someone screamed and we felt a rumble beneath our knees. The tiles cracked and a roar, gristly and deep, rolled out around us.

"What was that?" I cried.

Debbie shook her head, tearing her eyes away from Lewis. "This isn't good. He's too strong. Listen to me."

She pulled me against the receptionist's desk, and we climbed over, sitting underneath. The air was clearer here, and I could breathe and see without much effort. We pulled our masks down.

"You heard what he said," Debbie said. "His plan is to find a vessel strong enough to hold as much of him as possible. When Gaia, with the strength of Selene, destroyed Erebus and scattered him across the debris which became Earth, she didn't kill him. She just separated his body into billions of pieces. As those pieces come together, they grow in strength. Remember what we said. Erebus thrives off chaos. He wanted Francis Bateman as a host because he was rotten to the core. He could have withstood a large quantity of those split pieces. The more he has the stronger he is." I nodded to show I was listening. "But… he's spread himself thin by possessing all these people. He must know that we're capable of destroying them, because they're good people. They're not appropriate hosts." My dazed mind pictured Marley and Richards and I nodded in agreement.

"What are you saying?" I asked.

She thought for a moment.

"I think he has a source."

"A source?"

"Yeah. I don't know how. We know Erebus can survive in water and fire, because that's what the Earth was at one time. He can survive in those elements, or he wouldn't have ever been able to start coming back."

"So," I said slowly, trying to get it right, "do you think he has too many parts? He has too much stored somewhere and has nowhere to put it?"

She nodded.

"There has to be a hell of a lot in Taylor for him to be able to do the things he's doing, but it's not sustainable. He has to be keeping it somewhere. Somewhere close by."

I thought hard. "What are we looking for?"

"A fire that never goes out. Or maybe a large body of water that he can move?" I shook my head.

"None of those things are possible." I looked around and inhaled as a thought came to me. I peeked above the desk and saw, beyond the fighting, a water cooler and pipes leading into the wall. I sat back down and stared, wide eyed at Debbie.

"What is it?"

"He's in the building."

"What?"

"Think about it. Erebus possesses all these people but he's still one entity. One mind. Who knows how long he's been here? Richards and Marley, I can't see them anymore. What if they're protecting the source? What if

Erebus has been here longer than we knew? Feeding into it, pieces of itself? Bit by bit."

Debbie looked around at the walls. She ran her hand across the plaster, and then turned back to me.

"Where's the source?"

I pointed to a door across the room. "There's a water tank on the roof. The stairs are through there."

"Let's go," said Debbie. She stood, pulling me with her. We leaped over the desk and ran towards the door. Our way was blocked by a large woman. Debbie roundhouse kicked her in the chest, sending her flying back. Lois came from nowhere and jumped on the woman's back before she could recover, wielding her blade in the air and bringing it down in one movement, stabbing the woman in the chest. They fell to the floor and I saw as the decaying black tar of Erebus, seeped from her face. Lois righted herself and nodded at us. We nodded our thanks and she ran back into the fight.

We continued up towards the door. As we reached it and saw the green fire escape sign glowing above us, I turned and tried to see where James was. All I could see was the battle. Death and violence everywhere I turned. I tried to make out the bodies on the floor, praying none of them were him.

"Come on!" Debbie yelled, pulling at my sleeve. We opened the door and made our way up the stairs to the roof.

My eyes took a moment to adjust from the smoky setting to the florescence lights lighting the staircase. My improved stamina showed itself as we climbed the ten floors to the roof. Debbie led the way, our boots sending echoes around the shaft. I took off my jacket and let it fall over the edge of the railings, readjusting my grip on the Stiléto dagger.

When we reached the top, the door to the roof was already open and we were met with a cool summer breeze. My mind froze as we saw the large water tank looming over us, and I refused to believe what I was seeing. Richards and Marley stood either side of Carl Taylor. They had James, who was kneeling in front of them. His face had been beaten bloody and I couldn't tell if he was conscious.

"This is what you get for meddling in my business." Taylor's voice was barely above a whisper. Debbie and I slowly walked along the edge of the roof. I looked down and saw the warriors making their way out. The fight must have been nearing its end. I could see blue flashing lights in the distance.

I took a moment and then waved my dagger at Carl and my friends who now looked like corpses.

"If you touch him again, I'll kill you."

Carl smiled without humour and nodded to Marley and Richards. "You can't hurt us."

Richards started for me and Marley followed making their move on us, running head on, their feet sending the gravel flying. Debbie tried to put herself between us. A heroic move, I thought, but not necessary. I knew what to do. I knew what I *had* to do. I'd known it the moment Richards had snapped Becca's neck like she was nothing. I'd known it after looking into Marley's eyes. They were gone, or near as damn it. I looked at James and felt the weight on the shoulders of every Warrior. The choices they had to make. That *we* had to make. I was a Warrior. I accepted it and everything that came with that and as I did, I felt a rage burning inside of me as I pictured Richards and Marley's beautiful, alive faces. Free and kind and loving. James's beaten body floated into my vision.

I put my arm around Debbie's waist and spun her behind me, turning to face the officers I had emotionally detached myself from, so that what I did next wouldn't destroy me, and let fire erupt from my pores.

The flames felt cool against my skin and I barely noticed my clothes burn. Debbie jumped back and fell to the floor to avoid the heat. I turned to face her. I don't know what

163

my face expressed, but in her eyes, I saw the reflection of flames. An orange glow lit up the whole roof. Her mouth hung open and she laughed, which I saw as a good sign. Richards and Marley, however, were not laughing. I extended my hands and the flame ran across the floor, making its way up their bodies. Their screams were deafening, and I wasted no time in using my dagger. I leapt towards them in a single bound and plunged it into their chests. Two quick, precise stabs, one by one. No matter how hard I tried to tell myself that this was the kind thing to do, a piece of me still died with each fatal blow.

Their bodies fell to the floor, silent. I couldn't sustain the energy anymore and, as I let go of my hate, the flames extinguished. My clothes hung, torn and burnt, from my body. My skin was exposed around my legs, arms and stomach. I screamed at the agony of what I'd had to do and turned my anger to Carl.

"You're a mongrel," spat Carl. "The pathetic girl whose own planet I forced her to destroy, just so she could have a few billion years respite from my power.

"I am beyond you. I possess more strength than you could even fathom. I am everlasting. I have lived longer than time, and I will end you." I realised he'd seen in me the parts he couldn't explain. The reason he couldn't sense that I was a Warrior. "Selene. The goddess I overpowered before even Eden hung in the skies. This story is repeated. I destroyed them, and I'll destroy you."

I considered this. Had Selene been a goddess? Could it be that the asteroid that had created Eden had been Selene, a creation birthed from the attempt to destroy Erebus even before Gaia had been alive?

He was right. This story was on a loop. Would the same happen again? I gritted my teeth.

"I'm beyond *you,"* I told him, with a voice that felt like my own, but not quite. "You have no idea of my strength."

He laughed. "No idea of your strength?" He lifted his hand, a flame burned in his palm. My skin ran cold. "Where did you think you got that little trick from?" He extinguished the flame. "I wondered when I'd get to meet you. It's interesting to me that she'd pick you as the vessel to end me." He slowly walked back over to James. "You're fighting a fool's war, you know."

At that moment, the doors of the roof burst open and almost the entire Sina and Price clan stood behind me. I didn't know whether to be glad or not that Lewis had been the only fatality on our side.

They must have seen the light of the fire from the grounds below. They were bruised, blooded and exhausted, sure, but they were alive.

I turned, smug, to face Carl. "Lose, will we?" I was ready to fight him. Ready to throw him and myself off the ten-storey high roof top, if I had to.

I was not ready for what actually came next. I would never be ready.

Carl punched his fist through the water tank and a thick stream of blackened water drenched over James's head. He came to, opening his eyes and gasping at the cold. The blackness climbed up his body and evaporated into a cloud, before ramming its way into his open mouth.

"No!" I screamed. If seeing was believing then I resigned myself to the fact that I couldn't *not* believe. However, much I wished it wasn't, this was happening. This was very real and it had just ruined my life. James' body shook violently. I screamed again and tried to run for him. Debbie and Marcus grabbed me.

"He's dead, Lauren. He's gone. We need to go." I heard Debbie's words, but I ignored them. I watched as Carl rested his hand on James's face. The possession that had once controlled the drug dealer poured itself into the man I loved.

"Stop it!" I screamed.

Carl Taylor – the real Carl Taylor – stood, possession free, sweaty and confused. He had a second to breathe before James's body stood up. It sent an unseen wave of energy at Carl, hurling him off the roof. His body made a splat when it hit the ground.

Someone – I didn't know who – was pulling me back. The skin on James's face was peeling and flaking as his body struggled to contain the entity within him.

"No!" I cried. Tears streamed down my face.

"He's too strong now. We have to go."

James smashed his fist into the roof top. An ear-splitting *crack* and *crunch* rang around us as the building started to split.

He was going to take us down with it!

I didn't choose to leave, but I didn't fight them either. I allowed myself to be dragged away and down the staircase. I sobbed the whole way, but eventually found my feet.

A part of me hoped that the building would come down on me. Or on him. I wanted it to crush him under the weight of its bones. Because I knew that if he didn't die there, I would have to be the one to kill him.

Chapter Thirteen

I watched, numb, from the back window, as the station crumbled in parts to the ground. I couldn't see James anymore and didn't delude myself into pretending he'd gone down with the roof, like I knew Marley and Richards bodies would have.

The building that had been my second home was now reduced to a pile of rubble. Half of the station still stood, but the structural integrity was surely ruined.

We passed a line of police cars with their blue lights flashing and sirens wailing. Too late. The damage was done. James had been taken. More than twenty officers were dead, including two of the best people I'd ever known and I'd just discovered one of my greatest powers came from the evil entity that was trying to destroy my planet.

Inside the car was silent. The sirens faded into the distance and the engine hummed peacefully as though nothing in the world was wrong.

I looked out of the window on my left and saw a group of eighteen- or nineteen-year-olds, dressed in next to nothing, looking as sexy as they dared. They were drunk and laughing, falling into each other. I mourned my old life.

How long had it been? Two days? Three? It felt like a hundred. How long since I'd had my life taken from me and involuntarily donated to this cause? I guess it's my planet too. But why should I give a damn? Nobody tries to save the planet from Global Warming. Nobody fights to end unjust wars. I was tired and broken. I leaned my head against the glass and closed my eyes, letting the nausea of travel wash out the ache in my chest. Why couldn't somebody else do it?

I knew the answer, of course. Because nobody else would...

I could have opened the car door right there. I could have waited until we were on the motorway and at full speed, opened the door, taken off my seatbelt and let the wheels of the car drag me under. It was a tempting idea. So, what if I did? The world would surely end by the hands of Erebus, in a river of blood and chaos. Erebus would move on to the next world and go on winning, yet never satisfied in its inflicted misery.

No.

Fine.

If I had to find something to live for, let it be revenge. I'd fight for the Warriors. I'd join this war, but I would fight it my way. If they wanted a leader, I'd lead them. I'd take my revenge, but first I would free James. I just hoped I could find the strength to deliver the final blow in the way

I had for Richards and Marley. They had been my friends and I'd managed to do it...but James was – I swallowed back the lump that had risen in my throat.

I wasn't sure how long we'd been driving before we pulled off down a country lane, but I had started to lose feeling in my legs. I'd lost feeling everywhere. I felt like I should be crying but I just really wanted to go to sleep.
 We stopped in a dark passing place, sheltered from the stars by trees that branched out and held their neighbours overhead. It was Lois who opened my door. She held out a hand for me and I took it, letting her small frame support me as I slid from my seat. My boots landed softly on a raised bed of grass.
 I noticed Lois holding her side. There was a gaping wound and blood seeped through her fingers. I silently rested my hand on hers.
"I'll heal," she said.
"I'm sorry about Lewis." I whispered, realising that I wasn't the only one who had lost tonight. She smiled softly.
"He lost his wife in a battle fifty years ago...I like to think he's with her now." Water filled my eyes as I imagined James with his mother and Sensei Clarke all alone in the world.

Not yet. I blinked fast to stop my eyes from betraying me. He wasn't gone yet.

She led me round the car, and I followed the retreating figure of Marcus up a slope. We climbed through a row of barbed wire, and I ignored the pain as a piece shredded the skin on my arm.

It'll heal, I told myself. *I'll heal.*

A few steps ahead I could see the helicopters. Nicholas stood waiting. Debbie walked ahead and he embraced her. Their hands dug into each other's backs and each buried their heads in the other's shoulder. My hearing, however much I'd tried to ignore everything it picked up, heard Debbie mumble into his coat.

"Everything's changing."

Wasn't that the truth? He kissed her on the forehead, and she climbed into the helicopter, taking her seat up front by the pilot. Nicholas looked over at me. I stared back, not feeling anything, not showing anything. I didn't want to talk. I just wanted to sleep. I ached to my bones and I knew it wasn't from the fighting. I could literally feel the emptiness, the absence of James, manifesting in every atom of my being. A lump rose in my throat and I swallowed it down, refusing to submit to my emotions. If I let it out now, I doubted I'd ever stop.

Sheridan ran across to me. "You're in this one," he explained, pointing to the helicopter Debbie had climbed in to. I felt he had something more to say, so waited before taking my seat. He kicked a stone amongst the grass before finding the courage to say what he had to say.

"We'll be going somewhere different to you. It's safer if we split up for a bit."

"Okay," I nodded.

He hadn't finished.

"It means nothing, I know. I can't imagine anything we say will mean anything to you, but all the same, it was my honour to have met you and… I can't begin to express how sorry I am." He bowed his head and turned to join his group in the second helicopter. I think he knew I wouldn't have much of a response and I was grateful that he hadn't waited for one.

He was right. It had meant nothing.

I took my seat in the first helicopter. Marcus climbed in beside me, looking down the whole time. I fastened my belt over my shoulders and across my middle. His large frame offered a small amount of comfort and my position leant towards him, craving a warmth nobody but James could have provided.

Nicholas jumped in last and slid the door closed. He took a seat on the other side of me, not saying a word. There was a wave of guilt in the air. Everybody felt responsible, but none more than me. He should never have been there, and this was my fault.

The propellers started spinning. The face of a woman I had seen back at the house – an event that seemed a thousand years ago – and that I had seen fighting at the station, sat across from me. She wouldn't meet my gaze either.

I didn't think anybody would bother me with conversation, but I didn't want to risk it, so when everybody else put on their headphones, I left mine off. I allowed the deafening noise to hammer my eardrums and closed my eyes. I didn't mean to fall asleep, but the heaviness of my eyes pulled me under, and the darkness of dreamless unconsciousness gave me a welcome respite from my own, thoughts.

I woke to the feeling of the helicopter touching down. I tried to look outside the window, but it was pitch black and I didn't have the strength to try and focus on using the night vision I surely had.

Marcus unfastened his seatbelt and slid open the side door. When he turned to offer me a hand, it was the first time I had taken a good look at his face. His eyes were bloodshot and puffy, as though he had cried the whole flight back. I didn't want to share my pain, but it seemed he felt quite a bit himself. Most likely for his fallen family member, Lewis. I offered him a warm side smile and he winked, weakly, by way of thanks. I took his hand and stepped off the chopper onto grass.

I still couldn't see very much but I could smell a freshly mowed lawn and the poignant whiff of manure. We were not at the same house we'd left. No big manor with looming pillars or secret galleries. No large dining table or war rooms.

There were flickering lights in the distance and, as my eyes naturally adjusted, I could make out the silhouette of a cottage with candles in the windows to guide our way. I'd taken a few steps towards the small path ahead when a heavy hand held my shoulder to stop me.

"Can we have a moment alone?" Marcus asked.

I really just wanted to find a bed so I could go back to sleep and pretend the world wasn't a warzone, but as Debbie and Nicholas passed me, I saw a look in their eyes. They already knew what Marcus wanted to speak to me about and it was important enough that they weren't stopping for the conversation.

"Okay," I said.

We walked in silence for what felt like half an hour, but couldn't have been more than ten minutes, as when I'd turned around to see how far we'd walked, I could still see the cottage in the clearing.

We took a turn and Marcus led me down a small path. My foot knocked something on the ground. I had to double take.

A Stiléto was stuck into the earth. And another one beside it. I took a look around and my mouth dropped open as I saw that we were surrounded by them. There must have been over a hundred Stilétos, imbedded in random places, dotted around a slab at the centre of an open plane. We walked towards it, I watched my feet the whole time, making sure I didn't trip over any of the hilts.

Marcus rested his hand on the slab and sighed, a tear running down his cheek. The slab was covered in names.

"This is a graveyard," I said.

Or a memorial at least. I looked around again. These were the Stilétos of the fallen and the slab was marked with their names. That lump threatened to rise again, and I gulped it back down. Not here. Not yet.

Marcus turned to me and pulled something from his belt. He handed me a dagger. There was blood on the wavy blade, right up to the hilt.

"This is the one he used to save me," I said. Marcus nodded. I looked at the slab. The name Sina was everywhere. Marcus knelt at the stone and besides the name *Victoria Sina* he carved with another Stiléto, the name *Lewis Sina*. He then took the dagger and pushed it into the ground. He turned to look at me. My stomach twisted as I realised what he was trying to do for me.

"I can't," I said.

"Oh, but you can." Marcus stood and made his way back to the slab and stroked the names with his finger tip.

"But he wasn't a Warrior. He is… was human." Marcus shook his head.

"My dear, any human who would join our cause and fight the way he fought, who would lay down their life in battle, has a place here." He tapped the rock. It took me a minute, but after swallowing a few times and taking a deep breath, I kneeled to the ground and used the bloodied blade to carve his name into the slab.

PC James Clarke

It took a while as my hand shook and I wanted it to be as perfectly presented as the rest of them. My nose burned the whole time and I wiggled it to keep my tears from forming. When I'd finished, I stood and scrutinised my handiwork. It wasn't perfect, but it wasn't terrible. I looked around me and found an empty space. I balanced the tip of the blade on the soil and pushed until it was buried to the hilt. I stayed a moment, brushing my hand on the markings.

Marcus lifted what looked like a very old bottle from beside the slab of names and uncorked the top. It went *pop*. He sipped and I could tell it had to be strong stuff to make him grimace the way he did. He offered it out to me. I took it without hesitation and drank.

A sip was all I needed. The liquid was like fuel, burning the moment it touched my lips. I felt the hot nectar scald its way down my throat, hitting like a furnace in my stomach. I coughed violently and handed the bottle back to Marcus. He sipped it again, goodness knows why, and set it back in its spot.

"There is much to discuss. But that can wait until tomorrow. Tonight, we will sleep and, Selene willing, dream of nothing but good things." He rested his arm on my shoulder and steered me back towards the cottage. My heart felt fuller with the kindness he had bestowed on me. My stomach sloshing with enough liquor to put an elephant on its arse made me crave somewhere soft to lie my head.

When we entered the house, everybody had already made their way to their respective rooms. A tall lady led me to an open fire burning in a cosy front room. She sat me in a large, padded chair, which I sunk into. I untied my heavy-duty boots, and kicked them off my feet. Her husband, a short man with a bald head and hooded green eyes, handed me a pair of checked pyjamas.

"Come with me, my love. I'll show you to your room," the tall lady said, but I didn't stand.

"Do you have a phone?" I asked with barely enough energy to breathe.

I stood in the corner of the washroom; my bare feet cool on the tiled floor. It was a welcome change to the heat of the front room, which made me wonder how a family could survive with that lit fire on a summer's night. Their phone had a rotary dial and it took a few attempts to get the number right. I twisted the wire in my fingers, tangling and untangling as the phone rang out. I half hoped nobody would pick up.

No such luck.

There was a click and the familiar voice of Sensei Clarke greeted me.

"Hello." I didn't reply. "Hello?" he said again. "Anyone there?" I coughed to clear my throat.

"Lauren?" My eyes filled with tears. He could tell who I was just by that one noise. I blinked fast and took a deep breath.

"Yeah, it's me."

"Lauren!" he said, ecstatically pleased to hear from me. "How are you, how have you been? It's been a while since I heard from you. Is James with you?"

I bit my lip.

"No." I couldn't do it. What had I been thinking? What was I even supposed to say? "He's not with me right now." Not a lie. "I just... I just wanted to hear your voice." Also, not really a lie. He could sense something was off, though. Of course, he could. He'd basically raised me.

"Is everything alright, Lauren?" I bit my lip again, so hard I could taste blood.

"Uh-huh." My first lie. I leant my head against the wall beside me. "I... erm – you know what? I've just had quite a day and... I found myself thinking about everything you'd done for me and realising that I don't think I ever thanked you."

There was a pause on the other end. I could imagine him sitting there on his own big armchair, blinking back his own tears.

"You don't have to thank me for anything, Lauren. I'm proud to have had the pleasure of bringing you up in my home. You're like a daughter to me. You know, that right? And I love you like my own." I nodded even though he couldn't see me. I gulped.

"I just thought I should call and tell you that I'm grateful. I'm grateful to you and – and I know that James –" My voice caught in my throat as I said his name, "James is so proud of you too."

"Lauren, where is all of this coming from?" His voice was soft, and it made the whole thing so much harder.

"Thank you, for being my home. Thank you for not giving up on me when everybody else was tired of me and… thank you, just, you know, for being my dad."

There was a long silence and I thought for a moment that he'd hung up on me. I wondered if it actually *was* a bit too much. I heard a sniff and realised he had just been sat there, saying nothing, crying silently on the other end of the phone. I stayed there, holding the receiver to my ear, listening to his breathing and thinking of what James would have wanted. He would have wanted his dad to know all of that. Lawrence finally pulled himself together and managed to say a farewell.

"Love you, Lauren. You make me proud, kid." I smiled at the wall. A painful, twisted smile. "Tell James to give me a call, okay. I want to rub this in his face a little bit." He laughed and then I laughed.

"Bye," I whispered.

"See you soon, okay?" He hung up the phone and I walked away to find a place to crash, that one sip of liquor and today's traumas catching up with me at last.

Chapter Fourteen

The sunlight woke me up. It streamed through the white Venetian blinds and heated the room to an unbearable temperature. I'd crashed on top of the duvet at least, but still fully clothed.

There were voices coming from the garden. I pulled myself up, retying my hair into a bun on top of my head, frizzy red strands hanging down where it wouldn't reach the tie.

I peeked through the blinds and blinked back the penetrating rays. Debbie and Nicholas sat across from each other on patio furniture. They seemed deep in conversation. The tall lady placed a tray of juice on the table and they smiled their thanks.

There was a knock on the door.

"Come in," I croaked. The short, bald man opened the door.

"Oh good, you're up." He walked in and placed a change of clothes on the bed. A pair of shorts and a light vest top. It nearly brought a smile to my lips that these tough, muscular people always seemed to have a spare pair of clothes on hand, and they were always very much in style. I supposed that's what this kind of work required – common sense. I nodded thanks.

"The bathroom is down the hall. You'll find everything you need." He started to take his leave.

"I didn't catch your name."

He turned and smiled warmly. "Christian. And my wife, you met last night, her name is Lesley." I didn't think he looked like a Christian, more like a Paul or a Craig.

I waved, pathetically. "Nice to meet you."

"And you." He left, closing the door softly behind him.

After changing and washing, I made my way down a small creaky staircase. The cottage was straight out of a fairy tale, complete with low hanging beams, open fireplace and a crooked window with tiny blue birds resting on the sill.

The smell of coffee made my mouth salivate. The sound of a creaking floorboard turned me around at speed. Marcus stood, looming, in the doorway between the kitchen and the sitting room. He held up his hands in a *I-mean-no-harm* sort of way. My eyes still stung from last night's crying, and I blinked trying to stop the burning.

"Sorry," I mumbled, "I'm still a little jumpy." He came into the room, ducking under the beams.

"To be expected," he said. He picked up the coffee pot from the hot plate and poured two cups.

"Milk?" He asked.

"And sugar, please." He pulled out a spoon and dragged the sugar jar towards him, spinning off the lid.

"Two?"

"Three." He smiled broadly and turned his head to me.

"Me too." He served up the sugar and poured milk from a little white jug. The whole scene seemed surreal and perfectly normal, all at the same time. He handed me my cup and gestured for me to lead the way outside.

The garden was warm, and the sun beat down on my pale skin. I winced and took a seat on a stone step which led down into a field. I stared out at the open plane.

Birds tweeted in the trees. I could hear water running somewhere, signalling a brook nearby. When I focused, I could make out a small lake in the distance, just before a forest which surrounded the cottage and its land.

The day was lovely, and it irritated me. The clouds should have been smothering the summer sun and it should have been pouring with rain. The world should not go on spinning like that when a beautiful soul had been lost to the darkness.

Marcus sat down beside me. "Much to discuss?" I asked. To my relief, he shook his head.

"Not just yet." He whispered. "This morning, we will be grateful to be alive on such a beautiful day." I twisted my mouth.

"Not sure how I could do that, to be honest." He gently nudged me with his shoulder.

"You can. When the worst has happened, when we've lost everything, there will still always be this." He gestured around him. "An overly sweet coffee and a place to take in the view while we drink it."

I sipped my drink. It was good coffee. I inhaled deeply, the smell of the grass, the sweaty heat, Marcus's aftershave, the coffee. In spite of myself, I felt peaceful.

"You see?" He smiled. "There is always something to be grateful for. Enjoy these moments."

We sat in silence for an hour and I let the sun burn my fair skin and play with my freckles. I assumed my accelerated healing would deal with the sun damage.

When we finally stood up, it was because Lesley had brought us some food. She placed a tray of bacon, scones, teacakes, strawberries and toast on the table.

Nicholas and Debbie had already headed back inside before Marcus and I had come out, but they now reappeared for brunch.

The rest of the family pottered out from the house. Lois and a man from the helicopter who introduced himself as Clint, came from across the field, carrying long sticks. They were sweaty, and red in the face.

We all sat down around the patio, eating in silence. I bit into a piece of crunchy bacon and thought for a moment.

If I was to take my revenge, I would need to train. I was a fair fighter before all of this and I could handle myself generally, but this was a different league all together.

"Will you teach me?" I asked, not to any one person, but to the group as a whole. I figured I had a better chance of someone agreeing to train me if I asked them all.

I was met by an awkward silence. A blue bird tweeted overhead.

"I will train you." Marcus conceded. The group turned to stare at him. "Keep your hats on," he told them. I was confused.

"If I'm to fight with you now, then I'm going to need to be as good as all of you," I explained. More silence. "I'm confused. Why is it such a bad thing to teach me how to fight?"

Debbie cleared her throat.

"It's not. It's... we're... We're not staying here with you for very long. We thought it would be for the best if we handled... this situation first. Then we could move forward with training you." I looked around searching for a clearer answer in their faces.

"Situation?" Then it hit me. "James?" Debbie nodded.

"But I'm coming with you," I exclaimed, outraged. "I want to be the one to do this. None of you even knew him."

"That's exactly the point," Nicholas explained. "We can be free from emotion in our mission."

"We don't even know where he is yet," Lois interjected. "We're leaving with a team at noon to track his whereabouts."

I raised my eyebrows. "Is that so?"

"We won't make a move without you knowing beforehand, but it really is best if you sit this one out," Debbie pleaded.

I shook my head. "If you want me to fight with you in the war, I'll fight with you. If you want me to lead you, I'll lead you, but you have to respect me as such. Either I'm the one to do this —"

"*This* being, to kill the man you love," Debbie clarified.

I stopped. It seemed so much more real when somebody else said it. My lip wobbled.

"How about," Nicholas said, slowly, "I lead the tracking team. Debbie, you stay here with your father, start her training, and I give you my word… we will return here when we learn of James's whereabouts. We won't do anything before you know about it." He shrugged his shoulders. "Does that work?"

I suddenly felt like a spoiled brat, but I couldn't shake the feeling that he was lying. What could I do?

I nodded. "Thank you."

True to their word, Nicholas, Clint, Lois and – to my shock – Christian left at noon in a rather simple looking car. I'd half imagined them to fly away in a flashy, high-speed jet, but guessed if you were on a track-and-report mission, being inconspicuous was key. I knew Debbie had wanted to go with them and suspected she may have had concerns for Nicholas's welfare, but she had kissed him goodbye and led me to the training area without saying another word on the matter.

The training area resembled a tennis court without the markings. The floor was made of red clay and I could smell it burning in the heat, like rubber. Marcus was already waiting on the side-lines for us, and I nearly laughed when I saw that Lesley had pulled up a sun lounger to spectate.

I wondered why nobody had brought up my apparently Erebus-resembling ability to create fire. I decided they had probably discussed it in private and had a few things to say that they didn't think I would be ready for. I wondered what everybody knew about me that I didn't. I decided, for the time being, not to use these powers to my advantage. I wanted to learn the basics.

Marcus walked onto the clayed floor and met Debbie and me in the middle.

"I know you've had your fair share of training, Lauren, and I won't patronise you by trying to explain the physics of throwing a punch or the momentum you need to successfully pull of a round house kick. I want you to focus on your instincts. They're your greatest asset and you seem reluctant to trust them. A typical Warrior is born with the ability to use their strength, with the ability to see in the dark, to predict where a threat is coming from, to sense when an Erebus is near."

He suddenly backhanded me across the face, and I fell sideways onto the hot floor. I held my jaw and looked up at his looming figure.

"Obviously, there is something defective in these instincts." He walked a few steps away.

So that's how it was going to be. This is the treatment a Warrior received when he or she trains. Was this the kind of experiences they had from childhood, or did they wait for them to turn eighteen before the real violence began? I suspected the former.

I stood back up and put my hands behind my back, refusing to let them see me sweat.

"Blame it on what you will," he continued. "Obviously, there's something we've missed. Something about the darkness." He looked over to Lesley and conveyed a secret concern. Her lips were set in a hard, thin line. "It's possible you were sought out by a powerful part of Erebus, and he wiped your memories. But then wouldn't it have been easier to just kill you, if it knew who you would become?"

He stopped pacing. The questions had turned in on himself and he shook his shoulders, bringing himself back to the task at hand. I tried to meet Debbie's eyes but she stared at the ground, pretending she hadn't noticed his lapse.

"It's irrelevant for the time being. Our task is to bring those instincts back to you. We will push you until you feel like there are eyes in the back of your head. Until you feel like you can predict every move your opponent will make. Until it becomes second nature to watch your own back." He patted Debbie on the arm and took his leave to the edge of the court.

Debbie assumed a boxing stance and rounded on me. I mirrored her. She swung for me at full speed and I dodged, stepping sideways. She lunged again and I whacked her hand away before trying to land a kick on her side. She countered by booting me in the chest before I had a chance.

I skidded across the floor, my backside burning across the clay. I tried to stand before she had another chance but she was so much faster than me. She flew through the air, grabbed the scuff of my shirt, and flipped me, mid-jump, across the platform. She landed perfectly on her feet. I landed in a heap, the skin on my forearm peeling off. I looked up to see Debbie running towards me, not offering a moments respite. I could feel the blood trickling down my arm and Marcus shouted to me from the distance.

"You have strength, Lauren! Use it!"

I thought about James. I thought about how helpless I had been on the rooftop. I thought about the water flowing over his bruised face. The Erebus clawing its way down his throat. A rage bubbled inside of me and I let it run like a wildfire through my veins. My eyes seemed to focus on Debbie, and everything slowed to half its normal speed. I took in her stance, her momentum. I waited until she was right before me, not giving her a second to predict my next move.

I spun my legs from under my body and swept them under her feet. She flopped to the ground with a *thud*. I refused to give her a chance to recover and, from my floored position, I used her own move on her. I gripped her by the scuff of her shirt and spun us both, in one smooth motion, through the air. I released and watched as I landed and she continued to fly off the platform, rolling several times across the grass. I heard Marcus laugh.

"That's what I'm talking about!" he yelled. I looked down at the floor where I had landed and saw that my feet had damaged the clay underneath.

Debbie stood up and coughed. Scowling, she stormed back towards me. I enjoyed seeing this power in my new friend. The distraction was welcome, and I braced myself for her offense.

"Not bad," she said.

She reached into her back pocket and pulled out a silk scarf. She tied it around her eyes. Marcus came behind me and did the same thing to me. I was plunged into darkness.

Everything around me seemed louder. My breath, the scuffle of loose gravel on the clay platform as Marcus shifted to the side. The lounger creaked as Lesley leaned forwards. I heard a swish of air and felt a fist connect with my chin. The sounds muted and I fell, for the third time, to the floor.

"Ow." I rubbed my chin. My lip was busted. I could taste blood. Something made the hair on my neck stand up. I didn't know what was happening, but I knew it wouldn't be good. I spun around and caught Debbie's foot in my hands. The grooves of her trainers digging into my flesh. I shoved as hard as I could and felt the floor vibrate as she hit the ground, away from me.

"Good," I heard Marcus call. I scrambled to my feet and lost sense of which way I was facing. Something whacked into my back and I heard a pop as I crashed forward and my shoulder took the brunt of my fall. A painful pulsing began down my arm. My shoulder had come out of its socket!

"Argh!" I cried out, knowing nobody would come to help. This was how you learnt. I tried to focus on the sounds around me, instead of the pain. Not an easy thing to do. I gritted my teeth and stood up. I felt a pressure in my stomach as something made its way towards me. I stepped to the side and felt Debbie's body sweep past. She had used her full momentum and couldn't stop, so had tumbled over.

I took advantage of the chance and grabbed my arm, pulling it violently back into the socket with another pop. The pain disappeared in an instant and I took a sharp intake of air through my lips.

"Had enough yet?" Debbie taunted. She'd given away her position, right behind my left ear. I ducked to the ground as she'd reached for me, and felt her body topple over mine.

I stood up as her chest leaned on my shoulder and barged her up into the air. I spun around and waited until I sensed her body was at the right height, before lifting my hand, placing it on her stomach and slamming her into the ground. Everything shook and I was jolted into the air, slightly. When my feet landed again, I heard several cracks and noted the unevenness of the clay. Marcus whistled loudly and I removed my scarf.

The light was a shock to my sensitive retinas, and I blinked as everything sharpened. I looked down to see a Debbie-shaped crater in the ground. She lay inside the cracks and was removing her own blind fold, squinting. She groaned and held her rib.

"Had enough yet?" I joked. She smiled up at me and nodded, holding out her hand. I helped her stand back up and she limped out of her hole. Her leg was sticking out at an odd angle and she pushed the broken bone back into place with a grunt. She made it look so easy and I felt a smug bit of satisfaction that I'd bested her.

"That's the strength of the leader we've been waiting for," she panted. Marcus approached and patted Debbie on the back.

"Take five my dear." I started to follow, and he stopped me.

"Not you. You're not finished yet." He handed me a dagger, but it was not a Stiléto. It was a plain, metal knife. He pulled out another one for himself. I felt the weight and the cool handle in my hand.

"We've established, I believe, that our Stilétos can do you no harm. Which is wonderful, but it's doubtful that our enemy would use one of these anyway." He stepped back and my heart fell in my stomach as I realised, he meant for me to have a knife fight with him.

"But I can't." I gasped.

Marcus laughed. "But of course, you can." He lunged forward and swiped at me. I stepped back and the side of the blade cut me slightly across my top, a red streak of blood showing on the white fabric. I looked at him, my eyes wide.

"Problem?" he asked, a cheeky smile on his face. I clenched my teeth and ran at him. He grabbed my extended wrist, where the dagger was gripped within my fist and brought his own dagger up towards my sternum. "You're dead now." He dropped my wrist. "Watch yourself. You can afford to take a punch to the ribs, or even a kick to the face, but when weapons are in play, you keep your frame defended."

I watched him, the way he kept one arm always in front of his torso. I copied his stance.

"Good." He said, long and deep. "Very good."

He lunged for me again. I blocked it and used my own dagger to swipe up at his arm, drawing blood. He dropped his weapon and caught it with his left hand, before spinning around on his knees, jabbing out towards my back. I'd seen it coming and kicked out, bringing my foot down on his hand, trapping it on the ground. I brought my dagger down towards his head, in a mock way to prove I was about to kill him.

His speed was unmatched, however, and he swept his legs under his body, kicking up and knocking the dagger from my hand. I ran for it as fast as I could. An idea came to me. A divine move. I caught the hilt and, in the same movement, I swung around and threw it, gently, towards Marcus. I knew he'd be able to dodge it.

As predicted, he slid to his knees, leaning back, the blade flying over his head. I had lulled him into a false sense of security and the next thing he saw was me jumping over him, at Warrior speed, chasing the dagger. I grabbed my hand around it and felt the tell-tale goosebumps raising on my neck, warning me he was approaching my flank. I kneeled to the ground and stabbed backwards, feeling the dagger imbed into his muscled stomach. I pulled it out, so it wouldn't go in a dangerous depth and spun around in time to see his own dagger coming down on me.

I was prepared for this and grabbed his wrist, using his weight as his body came down on mine, I pushed, and lunged the blade towards his throat. He stopped in an instant, the sharp point millimetres from his jugular. We breathed heavily. A wide smile split across his face. Sweat trickled down his temple.

"Very nicely done," he said, before carefully sitting back and dropping his blade to the ground. "You could have killed me twice there." I sat up to catch my breath.

"Are you hurt?" I asked, pointing to where my dagger had stabbed through his abs. He pushed down on the bleeding.

"You could have kept going, for me." He looked at the blood on his fingers. "You'll find we heal from most things. It would take a full impaling to even warrant a trip to the hospital. Or, of course, some other deadly force. If you'd taken my head of, for example. That would be pretty hard to come back from." He laughed. I looked down at my own wounds and saw a faint red line where there had once been quite deep cuts.

"I see that."

Marcus stood up and pulled me with him. I was trying to stretch out a stitch when all of my hairs stood on end and a cold shiver ran down my spine. I spun around and instinctively caught something silver as it flew towards my face. I felt a sharp slice in my hand and looked down to see I had caught an airborne dagger by the blade.

Marcus turned around and we saw Lesley standing from her viewing spot, her arm outstretched from the throw. She shrugged her shoulders.

"Just checking." She cocked her head. "She'll do well." I dropped the knife to the ground and let my blood drip on the clay. Debbie clapped her hands from her spectators' position on the side lines.

"That was a lot of fun to watch. Can she kick Uncle Clint's arse when they return?" Marcus laughed and slapped me on the back.

"Beautifully done."

Chapter Fifteen

We'd practiced a few more moves throughout the day and only stopped when our wounds had stopped healing as quickly. By now, the day had cooled into the evening.

Lesley had prepared a vegetable broth and home-made crusty bread for our dinner. My body was grateful for the nutrients.

After we'd eaten, we sat in the sitting room around the open fire. There was something hypnotic in the flames. I sat on the floor with my back against a coffee table, staring at the deep orange glow. I could see now why they kept it lit, despite the summer heat. We had kept the windows open for fresh air. Our eyes saw more detail than the average eye. I practiced flicking my vision from one to the next. Night vision made the heat glow a brilliant red, when I blinked and focused on one particular log, I could see into each individual crack where the embers were lit up in specks. Every time the fire crackled, I'd watch as a piece of ash rose up and settled on the marble in front.

Marcus led the evening entertainment with a few war stories. There was a time he had fought an outbreak of Erebus possessions in an Australian prison. Nobody really knew for certain how so much had managed to gain entry, but it was his job to stop it from spreading.

I zoned out somewhere between the gruesome first death and the monumental last death but came in with my full attention when he went into detail about how he'd met his wife, Lorna, on a ship en route to Peru. They had not fallen in love during some epic battle, or after some successful mission. They were both taking a break after their own separate tasks had been completed, and were looking for a bit of enjoyment and culture. It was a simple meeting. No fireworks, no heroic rescue.

He had been trying to go down a set of stairs, she had been trying to go up and as their hands had touched each other's arm in a bid to move the other out of the way, sparks had flown. They'd sensed the Warrior connection the moment they'd gotten close, but those sparks were something else entirely.

It had been the start of a many centuries' long relationship, built on hard work and a deep level of love and devotion. He sounded like Sensei Clarke, when he spoke of his wife. I knew Marcus's wife was still alive, but you could tell he missed her terribly, wherever she may be. He didn't offer up the information, so I didn't ask.

I focused again on the fire, looking desperately for a distraction. My brain wouldn't allow it and every thought I could spare was for a memory of Richards and Marley. Of playful banter and late-night takeaways. Of his brutal sarcasm and her gentle soul. What a waste of life. The guilt burned within me.

And then there was him.

We'd lit a fire once, on a beach. James and me. It was after we'd finished our twenty-two weeks training for the force. The whole experience had been quite drawn out and, when the rest of the class had gone out into town to celebrate with shots of sickly-sweet Sambuca, James had suggested we host our own party, just the two of us.

I would have followed him anywhere and so we jumped in his car and drove to the coast. There was no one around for miles. We sat on a rock and waited for the tide to come back in. It had been October at the time and the weather was bitter. James lit a fire using some dried debris that had washed ashore. We talked about anything and everything, about life and death. We'd laughed about relationships that had failed and cried about the mothers we would never know.

It had been a simple trip. We'd watched as the tide came in and started to surround us, forcing us to make our way back to the raised pier. The night rolled in quickly and freezing cold rain had drenched us. We'd danced in it, being silly. Being kids. It was one of the best nights of my life. Something I longed to relive.

The fire popped again and I could hear my bed calling for me. I took my leave, waving goodnight to the remaining Warriors and made my way up the rickety stairs.

The chatter amongst the family faded to silence as I gently closed the door. Lesley had laid out a long white night dress and I picked it up from the dresser. The cotton was soft. Everything this family gave me to wear was luxurious. I wondered if that was something they offered themselves for a job well done. Fine foods and fine clothing.

"They deserve it," I murmured aloud.

I stripped off my sweat and blood-stained shorts and vest and dropped them in the wash basket. The Venetian blinds were open, and I pulled the nightie over my head as I walked across to the window. The fabric clung to my bust and swished around my ankles. I pulled my hair down from its tie and let the wild waves bounce over my shoulders. I wasn't ashamed of how I looked any more. There was something pure about all of this. A basic instinct, reverting my mind back to its primal needs. The need to survive. To fight, to feed, to rest. It was a form of autopilot, I supposed, but there it was. We do what we need to do to get through trauma.

I opened the window and looked out into the expanse of wilderness. The fairy lights remained lit in the garden below, but they seemed dull in comparison to the moon. I could see it in such vivid detail, despite the late hour and the darkened sky. It almost looked like an eclipse to me now. The darker side was an admiral blue and the moon was so bright, it almost appeared white. The craters and the iced seas appeared richer to me. Their outlines a stark contrast. I tried to imagine that it had once been its own being. A part of another world.

That feeling of oneness came over me again. I closed my eyes and let the summer breeze clear away the hostilities of the day. My body had healed and yet it still ached. Everything still ached for *him*.

I took myself to my bed and hid underneath the duvet. I closed my eyes and wished for a dreamless sleep.

Something else happened instead. A dream happened. At least, I think it was a dream. It had felt real and kind of wonderful, with the potential of becoming a nightmare if I'd have let it.

My eyes opened to a forest. Rays of sunlight trickled through the trees. Butterflies fluttered by my face and I could hear the laughter of a child. I looked down. I was still wearing my long, white nightie and was barefoot. It didn't bother me much. The floor felt like carpet beneath my feet.

The air smelled of roses and everywhere I looked there was a colourful flower I couldn't name. It reminded me of the room at the Sina house. The one with the painting of the prophecy.

I started walking, letting my fingertips brush the foliage. I stopped at a large tree. I placed my hand on the trunk. I could feel the life force running through it. Clean, pure of soul. The spirit of the tree tickled my skin. I was suddenly aware of the life everywhere. I could feel it all. I could connect with it. A single bud hung from a green stem. I kneeled behind it and examined the colours. It was yellow at first glance, but the closer I looked, I could make out purple veins, connecting the plant to its water source in the stem. I placed my hand around it and let a light fill me up.

I focused it on the flower and, when I exhaled, the light flowed through me and its petals unfurled by the dozens. Petals and petals, until it resembled a hydrangea, but not like any I had ever seen. I sniffed it. It smelled like aftershave. The same kind James liked to wear on special occasions. I heard the laughter of a child again. It seemed closer this time. I turned around to find the source. A flicker of bright blonde hair moved through the trees. I followed.

"Hello!" I called after the child. "You don't have to be afraid of me. I won't hurt you." I saw her peeking out from behind a trunk. The face of a young girl with a skirt made of wheat. Her eyes were the colour of the sky.

"Gaia?" I breathed. The little girl ran.

"Wait!" I shouted. I ran after her to no success. The laughter ceased. I stood in the middle of the forest, not daring to move in case I missed her running by. I could hear something else. Not a child running, but water. I followed the sound until I reached a creek. There were pebbles everywhere, glistening under the scattered sunlight. I stepped into the water and let it run over my bare feet. A welcome, refreshing, burst of hydration in the heat. I followed the water with my eyes. The creek grew wider and deeper the further along it flowed.

My eyes caught a glimpse of blonde hair and I heard a splash as the little girl disappeared. I realised in my horror that she had fallen in. I stepped out of the creek and ran down the water's edge, jumping over fallen logs and larger boulders, searching the water for a glimpse of the little girl.

I came into a clearing and found myself at a lakeside. A woman screamed to my right, causing me to turn. Two women stood at the waterfront. They pointed to where the little blonde girl had just vanished beneath the surface. They called for help and, although people were coming, I was closer. I slipped out of my dress so it wouldn't weigh me down and jumped into the lake.

My eyes didn't sting in the slightest and I didn't struggle to find air. I stopped swimming and let myself sink, deep below the surface. I looked around for the girl but could see nothing but tall pieces of plant life, reaching up from the depths of the lake. I looked up and saw the sunlight split into a million pieces as it bounced off the ripples where the water met the air. The sun seemed to move across the sky and set all of a sudden. I was plunged into darkness.

I closed my eyes and said a silent prayer. A light disturbed me. I opened my eyes again and saw a glowing ball, rising from below. It stopped in front of my face and lit the whole lake.

There she was.

"Gaia." I thought. She heard me. She reached out her hands and held my face. I could hear her thoughts in my head. Different to the voice I'd heard earlier. The voice of Selene had been like a wise grandmother, with the vocal cords of a young woman. Gaia, in my mind, spoke as the little girl she was.

You have to find me. I held my hands over hers. *I have found you.* I thought back. She smiled at me and shook her head. She tapped the skin over my heart.

I'm with you. A part of you. Theia, you have to find me there.

I furrowed my brow. *But I'm not Theia. I'm Lauren. Lauren Smith. No parents. No blood family. No family at all, now. Are you sure everyone hasn't got the wrong person?* I asked of the girl.

She pointed to the lake above and the moonlight broke through the waters.

I left her to watch over you. She leads you now. Let her guide you to me. A tear trickled down my face and I wondered how it was possible underwater. It turned to ice on my cheek. *You are the girl with the false name. Discover who you are, so you can discover who you are meant to be.* There was something serene in her eyes. A bottomless blue I could have sunk into and stayed there for eternity. Gaia brought me peace. I didn't want to leave. Didn't want to find myself alone again, in that room, where James was not, lost in a world I didn't recognise.

Gaia started to rise to the surface, but I remained.

"Don't leave me!" I cried.

I'm with you always, Theia, she thought. *We are with you always.* She disappeared with the light and I was, once again, alone in the lake.

"Theia!" I heard someone call. *Theia?* "Theia!"

That's not me! I protested in my mind. Then my air ran out and I choked as my lungs nearly exploded and my mouth filled with water.

"Lauren!" That's my name. Who was calling me? I blinked and saw the water I was in had changed. It was murkier than it had been and seaweeds tangled my ankles. I closed my eyes tightly, begging myself to wake up.

"Lauren!" I heard again.

The voice sounded familiar, despite it being lost in the waters. An arm wrapped around my naked body and the next time I opened my eyes was on the bank of a small lake, lying on grass. I coughed violently, water spilling from my lungs.

"There you go." I opened my eyes, gasping for air and looked into the face of Nicholas. He wrapped me up in a long coat and I pulled it closer around me. The night was still warm, but the water had been so cold. I coughed again, this time my lungs seemed free from water. I took a few deep breaths as Nicholas rubbed his hands over my arms for warmth. I realised he was dripping wet. A car, with its doors open and headlights still on, pointed towards us.

"What were you thinking?" he asked when he was sure I was okay. I shook my head.

"Wasn't thinking." I wasn't really sure what had happened. "I think I sleepwalked."

He shook his head. "Is that something you do? Sleepwalk into lakes, naked?" I realised I'd somehow lost my nightie. My cheeks flushed, red hot.

"I'm so sorry." I gasped. "No. I don't usually."

"Just add it to your list of weird, huh?" he asked, that Swedish accent coming through stronger under the stress. I laughed. The sound of footsteps pounding on the grass grew closer. Lois led Debbie to us. She must have gone to the house to find her, when Nicholas had jumped in after me.

"What the hell happened?" Debbie exclaimed. She held my nightie in her hands and Lois held a bunch of towels and blankets. "I found this on the patio." She held up the nightie. I shook my head again and Nicholas answered for me.

"Sleepwalking," he said and I could feel him shrug his shoulders to Debbie. Lois wrapped a large towel around my shoulders and offered one to Nicholas. He declined and stood to let Lois take over. She dabbed at my dripping wet hair.

I watched, through my periphery, as Debbie grabbed Nicholas and kissed him deeply. When they separated, he pulled her into a hug.

"I just saw her running along the grass, naked as a new-born baby. I couldn't believe it when she jumped in the lake." He broke the embrace. "We waited for her to surface, but when she didn't… I panicked." Debbie picked up a towel from the floor and draped it over her husband's shoulders.

"It's okay," she whispered. I felt embarrassed for more reasons than I could count. I couldn't imagine where my mind would have gone if I'd caught my husband trying to warm up a wet, naked woman.

What on Earth was happening to me? I had to take every experience at face value. I had assumed Debbie stabbing me in the chest had been a nightmare, and that had actually happened. Had I had a vision? Were those forests the forests of Eden and was Gaia really here just now, in my mind, offering me words of encouragement and advice?

Find me, she had said. Find her where? I put a hand over my heart where she had pointed. There was nothing there except the empty ache that James had left behind.

My stomach lurched as everything came crashing back to me. The realisation of what was before me had dawned late, but it was here now, and I needed to know.

I scrambled up from my spot on the ground. Nicholas spun so his back was towards me as I threw my nightie over my head and put his jacket over that to conceal myself more.

"What are you doing back?" I asked when I was decent. Nicholas turned and put his arm around Debbie's shoulder. He squeezed tightly and took a deep breath in before nodding.

"You know why I'm back," he said, barely above a whisper. I dared not believe it, and everything else so far had been like a big game of Guess Who. I bit my lip and blinked back tears.

"I'm going to need to hear you say it." I don't think I was really prepared to hear it, but sometimes taking things as straight as you can, is the best way forward. He nodded and looked at Debbie as he answered.

"We found Erebus." He looked up at me and my heart felt like it had stopped beating. He clarified for my desperate face.

"We found James."

Chapter Sixteen

I couldn't believe it was still a discussion. I was certain that it had been agreed – I would go on the mission. I would be the one to free James. Apparently, there was still some confusion.

"I have major concerns about this," Nicholas was saying. "It's one thing to risk failing in the task at hand. It's a whole different thing to risk her life."

"But surely that decision should be left to me." I countered. I sat by the fire, dressed back in my nightie and wrapped in layers of towels and blankets. Lois sat behind me, still trying to detangle and dry my hair.

"Please, Lauren." He begged. "I'm not trying to hurt you. I want to give you what you want, but you're not going to be able to deliver the final blow that you think you can." He looked to his wife. "Please tell her." Debbie held up her hands.

"My love, you know I will agree with you until the day I die. I *do* agree with you, but I also have to confess that what Lauren is saying also makes sense. If we could be possessed by Erebus, and thank Gaia we can't, and it was you who had been taken over…" She shuddered. Nicholas reached out and took her hand.

"I know… I would want the same thing," he admitted. "But… if you had been the one. If you were the prophesized Warrior, the one everybody throughout our whole history had been waiting for... that would change everything."

Debbie nodded. "You're right, it would. But would it change the way I felt?" There was silence. Nicholas collapsed to his knees in front of her, where she sat on an armchair. The glow of the fire illuminated their faces and created dancing silhouettes up the walls. They were so beautiful to me and I hated to cause this conflict. I just hated the idea of James dying somewhere where I couldn't hold him. That was the thing, I realised. I took a deep breath, prepared to give an inch and hope they wouldn't take a mile.

"What about a compromise?"

All the heads in the room turned to look at me, wondering what I might say. Marcus had joined the party when we'd returned from my swimming trip. He stood, silent, in the corner of the room. Clint had gone into the kitchen to help Christian and Lesley prepare some drinks. I had a small audience and hoped, if they'd agree to my terms, nobody else would enter into the conversation with a counteroffer. I spoke to Debbie, realising she would be the best bet.

"You let me come with you... and I'll stay out of the way. Somebody else can be the one to... somebody else can do it. But you let me be there with him. I don't want him to be alone." I thought I might be sick. I couldn't believe I was having this conversation. I felt like a dog owner discussing having my beloved pet put down. That's essentially what was going on. James was suffering and we were offering a kindness to relieve this suffering. Nothing about this was fair. In my mind, I would most likely end my life with him, if I couldn't find the strength to carry on fighting.

The messages conflicted in my head. Stop or go on? Go on without James? I had to remind myself he was already gone. I wondered if, when he was really gone, I'd be allowed the time to mourn.

Nicholas rubbed his chin, still kneeling before Debbie. She reached out and stroked his hair. His eyes bore into hers, begging her not to agree. She looked up at me and I just hoped that my eyes begged harder.

They did.

She nodded her head. Nicholas slumped forward, resting his forehead on her lap. He sighed.

"My love," he said, sounding defeated. "This will prove to be a mistake." I sensed the conversation wasn't over for them but decided this would be the perfect time to take my leave. I thanked Lois for helping me smooth out my hair, declining her offer to braid it.

"When do we leave?"

Nicholas attempted to answer, but Debbie rested her hand on his shoulder to stop him. Perhaps she was afraid he would make an offhanded comment about how I wouldn't be leaving anywhere.

"We have to wait," she explained. "He is too strong for the numbers we have, and we had to split up to put as much distance between us and him as we could. It'll take time to gather everyone back together. We'll leave at sunrise. Try and get as much sleep as you can." I nodded my thanks and turned to leave. Another question popped into my head.

"Where did you find him in the end?" I asked. Nicholas cleared his throat and took a minute to respond.

"Not too far from the station." He answered, vaguely. I suspected he was concerned I would leave in the darkness, when everyone was sleeping, and try to take him on myself. That was exactly what I had been planning. His answer annoyed me, but I understood.

I took my leave and headed back up the stairs, to take Debbie's advice and try to get some sleep.

I heard an engine start. My eyes flew open and I looked towards the window. The only light in the room was from the moon outside, shining between the slots of the Venetian blind. I feared I was in the middle of another sleepwalking episode and pinched my arm to be sure I was awake. The pinch hurt and left a harsh red circle on my skin.

I pulled back my duvet and tiptoed across the room to the window. I could hear quiet chatter and recognised Lois's voice.

"This doesn't feel right." She sounded distressed.

"I agree, but you can't deny that this is for the best." That was Marcus.

"We should at least leave a note," she countered. I realised what was happening and I was furious.

"Lesley and Christian will take care of her in the morning."

"I pity the poor couple. She'll probably tear the place apart when she finds out."

I liked Lois. Despite her betrayal she had me down to the letter. I would, indeed, be tearing the place apart.

But it wouldn't be in the morning.

I tore over to the door and pulled hard on the knob, expecting it to fly open and bang on the wall behind. I wanted it to be loud so everybody would know how angry I was at their daring to go behind my back.

The door didn't move. It was locked. I pulled hard and felt irritated that my Warrior strength wasn't enough to break what must have been a very old lock.

I grabbed the knob, lifted my feet onto the wall and leaned back, pulling with all my body weight. I heard a body shift outside, and my rage grew when I realised somebody was holding the door on the other side.

That made a lot more sense. It wasn't just locked. There was one, maybe two, other Warriors behind the door as insurance. It was probably Lesley and Christian.

I heard someone say, "We may have a problem." It was, indeed, Lesley and Christian.

"Let me out!" I yelled. "What the hell are you playing at? Let me out!" I hammered on the door. "You're being ridiculous. You lied to me! How could you do this to me?" I asked, choking back tears. "Let – me – out!"

When I realised the door wasn't going to budge, I started to toy with the idea of burning the place down with my powers, but then decided against it. I didn't want to use that thing until I knew exactly where it came from.

I wondered if I could use brute force. I was stronger than them. But I was so tired. So, so tired. Everything had taken its toll on me, and sure, that was probably one of the reasons they didn't want me along in the first place.

My mind was made up. I was going. And I'd do whatever needed to be done to get there.

I turned around and looked at the window. I lifted the blinds and saw two vehicles driving away from the cottage. The red rear lights were like red flags to a bull. I growled in my throat. The window wouldn't open wide enough for me to fit through. Fine. I decided to take the hard route.

I played the day's events over in my mind as I tied my boots onto my feet, as tight as I could. I'd taken a beating. I'd been slashed and broken. And I'd healed. I would heal. I kept reassuring myself, making sure I believed what I was saying was true. I would heal. I took several steps back and leaned against the far wall. I could hear Lesley and Christian moving outside. I think they'd realised their mistake the moment I'd come up with an alternative escape route.

"I understand why you're doing this. But I love him, and I have to be the one to save him," I called to the couple. I felt guilty for the damage I was about to inflict. The door clicked open just as I started my run. I flew at the window and jumped into the air, shoving my full force into the impact.

The glass and the wooden frame shattered on the collision and my stomach fell from beneath me as I descended to the floor, two stories below. I hit the patio with a crunch. I had managed to adjust my landing, so my feet hit the ground before my head had, but as I tumbled forwards, I felt the bones in my leg snap.

I screamed out and looked down, pulling the nightie above my knees. I had angry, bloodied gashes across both my legs and a large bump on both sides where the bone was pushing into my flesh. I crunched down on my teeth as I pushed the bones back into place so they could heal. It was agonising and I was once again filled with the rage of their betrayal. The pain subsided swiftly, and I watched, in a state of awe, as the skin knitted back together, before my very eyes. The stinging in my ankles disappeared and I inhaled the summer night air. Looking up, I could see Lesley and Christian leaning out of the window, at the destruction below.

"I'll pay for the damage," I called up.

"My dear girl, you really should stay," Christian hollered. I shook my head and stood up, brushing off the glass. I turned to see where the vehicles were. They had stopped and must have seen my great escape. They didn't wait long, and the brake lights dimmed as they proceeded towards the road beyond the line of trees.

I didn't have time to delay.

"You understand, don't you?" I didn't know why it was so important to me that they did. I supposed growing up without a family leaves a need to hold the people who are good to you as close as possible. I heard Lesley chuckle.

"You'll do well my girl. I thought the whole plan was a little ridiculous if I'm being completely honest." She turned to Christian. "Don't pretend you didn't too." Christian shrugged.

"I tend to go with the majority. Just go, go!" I waved my thanks and took off sprinting after the cars.

The grass felt like air underneath my boots. My nightie had tucked itself between my legs and I pushed as hard as I could to catch up with them. I had to think a little smarter. There was no way I'd catch them this way. I waited until they turned and I knew the direction they'd be driving.

They went left. Perfect. I turned towards the trees, where I knew the road passed and headed straight towards it. I tried to keep my eyes on the headlights of the cars as they made their way up the path. It was unclear if they knew exactly where I was, or that I'd figured out how to get to them, but I kept going. My lungs burned as my body's need for oxygen went up. I let the rage carry me and my legs ran at a speed I never would have been able to reach in the past. My Warrior strength was finally coming through for me.

The lights grew brighter and I leaned my body forwards for momentum. I reached the tree line and barged straight through the low wooden fence, sending splinters shattering over the floor.

More clean-up for Lesley and Christian.

I skidded to a halt on the cobbled road, just as the front vehicle drove towards me. I could hear the driver hit the brakes and the tyres crunched violently as they tried to make an emergency stop. I realised they wouldn't be able to.

I could have moved backwards, I could have stepped to the side, but I wanted to use the situation as a show of power. I wanted them to see who I was. Because that was the thing. I was supposed to be their leader. That's what they wanted. They were asking me to give my life to their cause… and I supposed it was my cause too, but all the same. My life had been alright before Debbie had plunged that dagger into my heart. They couldn't have the best of both worlds. This was all I'd asked for.

I narrowed my eyes and reached out my hand. A surge raced through my body, reaching out to all my muscles. The car struck. My hand crushed a steel front barrier, which wove around the headlights. It clinked and screeched under my force. I didn't budge a muscle. The car came to a halt as it tilted forward slightly upon stopping, the back two tyres lifted a touch off the ground and landed back again with a plump bounce.

I stood back, straight, releasing my hand from the bumper. There was silence. My hair was knotted from the breeze of my run. I could feel the clammy stick of my sweat on my face and chest. I knew I must have had glass over my clothes and dirt goodness knows where. I must have looked a mess, basically.

"And where the hell do you think you're going?" I asked as I blinked through the headlight beams. I slowly made my way around the vehicle and opened the back door. I saw Sheridan and realised they must have been on their way to the cottage the moment Nicholas and his team had found James. I nodded hello. He lifted his hand and waved pathetically, his mouth hanging open. I looked over him and saw Lois in the far side. She had a very wide smile on her face, and I tried not to laugh. She must have enjoyed the show.

I climbed over Sheridan, making a big fuss to shove over his body, and plonked myself in the middle seat. I looked into the front and saw Debbie was driving, with Nicholas in the front passenger seat.

"Hi, guys," I said, as nonchalantly as possible. I clicked my seatbelt into place. "Nice night for it," I said, snuggling into my seat.

I looked down and saw my blood-stained dress and started picking off the tiny shards of glass. Nicholas turned ever so slightly in his seat. He didn't meet my gaze, but I knew he was looking in his periphery. He shook his head and looked at Debbie. Debbie shrugged her shoulders.

"You can't say we didn't try." She was right there. She put the car into gear and set off. "This car is new," she grunted.

I half expected Nicholas to start chewing my ear off, but instead, he took off his jacket and passed it back to me. I put it on over my nightie.

"Thanks," I murmured.

"Don't mention it," he grumbled.

Lois burst out laughing. I know Nicholas and Debbie would have been trying to convey their distain at my dramatic escape and pursuit, but when Sheridan started laughing too, they gave away their smiles.

The rest of the journey passed in a comfortable silence. I thought of the memorial. All those names and all those Stilétos. This family had lost a lot. I guessed in a life where you could die any day, you couldn't afford to stay mad at one another. You had to do the job and enjoy who you did the job with. I leant my head against the headrest and wondered if they would let me stay with them.

One thing was for certain. I was not going back home. The old me was dead. The me who had been a foster child, the me who had worked towards being a Police Officer for years, the me who was proud to wear that uniform, the me who was in love with her best friend and had been too damned cowardly to do anything about it... she was dead and I wouldn't miss her. I had planned on saying goodbye to all of that the moment I said goodbye to James.

My throat burned, my eyes prickled, and I closed them for a moment, imagining his face and wondering if any part of him remained. Wondering if his trapped subconscious would be able to see me while I held him in my arms. I wondered if he would forgive me.

The car took a sudden turn and I realised where we were. *Of course, it would be here.* Where else should this end, if not where it all began?
 The yellow blossom tree trickled its petals onto the floor, where I knew, if I looked, I would see a dry puddle of my blood. The *Marques Gym* sign lit up under the white floodlights. We pulled to a halt and every inch of my body yearned for the man who stood in the open shuttered doorway.
 The warm feeling was instantly squashed by the feeling of oil being poured over my skin as the warning of Erebus put my Warrior instincts into overload. The car tensed. James's eyes bore into mine. He looked right at me, smiled with no humour, and confidently turned his back on us, heading back inside the gym.
 He was expecting us.

Chapter Seventeen

"Stay in the car," Nicholas ordered.

Debbie snorted. "She's no safer out here alone than she is in there with us." Nicholas sighed harshly. He turned and looked at my nightie and rolled his eyes.

"If you weren't the Saviour of us all, I'd slap you," he snarled, before he jumped out of the car and slammed the door shut. Debbie smiled warmly at me.

"He's scared for you. You have to appreciate that we are a lot older than we look. You've already become like a child to us." I felt a tug in my chest. I smiled at her.

Lois laughed. "Am *I* like a child to you too?"

"My love, your father is like a child to me, because he is." I turned and looked at Lois. She was Debbie and Nicholas's granddaughter, after all.

"Come on, Lauren. Let's kick some Erebus arse." She elbowed my shoulder playfully and opened the door for us.

The car park was a familiar territory and it seemed criminal that I was standing here under these circumstances. A bitter taste tingled on my tongue. It pained me when I realised Erebus must have had access to James's memories for him to know to come here.

What was he planning? He knew who I was now. He knew my purpose, knew that I had the soul and the power of Selene inside me. He knew that I was built from the flesh of Gaia. Did he know that her soul, too, was a part of mine? Not that I had a clue how to let that part of myself out to play, but she was there. My dream had confirmed as much. I hadn't had time to discuss it with anybody and wondered if I ever should. I'm sure the moment for conversation would arise at some point, but now was not that moment.

Then there was the question: Who was Theia? My mind raced. Everything seemed to boil down to each individual moment I experienced and every time I thought I was getting closer to some great revelation, another question mark appeared in the place of clarity. There was always something more. Always something to add to the overload of information. A new skill, a new page in the history book, a new name, a new face, a new trauma, a new problem to add to the ever-growing pile of problems. My heart raced as fast as my mind.

I realised I was stalling. How ironic. I really didn't want to go inside. I didn't want to face him. The way he'd waited for us. There was something, that just didn't feel right. Of course, it didn't feel right. James had been possessed and the only way to free him was to kill him.

A lump rose in my throat and I vomited, behind the back of the car. A hand patted my back. A large hand. Marcus leaned towards me.

"That's it, kid. Get it up." He patted me again.

"I'm sorry." I managed to gasp between wretches. I was embarrassed. I was supposed to be strong now. Strong for James. Strong for myself. I was supposed to be proving a point. What an impressive leader I was turning out to be. Nobody listened to me. I was flaky. My prowess came and went. I really was a mess.

Marcus chuckled low. "It's alright. You'll get used to it. The presence of Erebus is overwhelmingly strong. There's a lot of energy here and you can feel it. It's nauseating to all of us... we've just adapted to the feeling. It'll pass." That explained a lot. My skin did feel particularly greasy. I inhaled through my nose and out through my mouth. I tried to suppress the feeling of being on the Teacup ride at a traveling fair and stood up straight, wiping the remnants off my chin.

"At a girl." He smiled and I gave him a weak smile back. He handed me a Stiléto which I took slowly. "You can do this. I know what they said. But if you get an opening... take it." He kissed me on my forehead and we turned to the group.

The numbers weren't great given how badly we had been beaten last time we had faced Erebus. Lois, Sheridan,

Clint, Debbie, Nicholas, Marcus, two men called Ainsley and Fredrick who were undeniably twin brothers and another female called Sarah, who was just as breathtakingly beautiful as her mother. I could see the striking resemblance as they stood next to each other. The dark, curled hair, the brown eyes with the green flecks. They were a strong bunch, but I feared it wouldn't be enough. We certainly didn't have the element of surprise and I wondered, idly, what on Earth we were waiting for.

"What are we waiting for?" I asked. Marcus rubbed his neck and looked to the top road. I followed his gaze. Was he waiting for someone?

"I guess we should make a move. Can't keep the parasite waiting."

The parasite. A parasite. It's a trick. A mirage. These are the things I told myself as we took the short walk across the car park, towards the gym. The cooler nights, slowly starting to trickle in.

We reached the threshold and moved as one unit. I was in the middle and figured it hadn't been a coincidence that I'd ended up there. Even if James had been stood right in front of us, I would have no way of getting to him and he would have had to go through nine other Warriors to get to me.

"Well, don't we look cute?"

The voice coming out of James's body echoed out around the gym. My skin tingled. It was his voice, but not his voice. It was colder. The emotion sounded fake. I followed where it came from and saw James standing on the edge of the boxing ring, leaning against the ropes.

"Look at all of you, huddled together like penguins!" He tutted. "Let me see her." Nobody moved. "Let me see her," he asked again, a hint of tension in his tone. Nobody moved. James, or Erebus, jumped down off the platform and waved his hand.

That was all he did. Just a wave of his hand and the Warriors around me parted, the way cars did when we rode in the Police car with the sirens on. They slid into the surrounding walls and gym equipment. I heard a few grunts and moans as a few heads took the brunt of the fall.

I felt cold. He was so powerful. James was on me and as I saw the Warriors start to stand, I held up my hand. For once, they listened to me. I knew this may have happened. I'd kept the Stiléto in my hand the whole time and I was surprised he'd dared get so close. But he wasn't stupid. He had James's memories.

As he stepped closer towards me, I couldn't see him as the entity everybody feared. I couldn't see him as anything but James.

Then, something about him made my stomach lurch. His skin. His skin was peeling all over. I'd seen a corpse once, over a week old, and it had not been kept fresh. This was like that. I realised why. It was the same thing we'd seen during the battle at the station.

"You made a mistake taking James as your host," I told him, a definite quiver in my words. James tilted his head.

"Do you think I'm afraid of you, little girl?"

"Actually, I do," I told him, not blinking. "Can't you feel it, though? The decaying of his body?" He looked down at the back of his hands, where the skin was starting to mottle, and he snarled at me.

"That's right," I continued. "You picked one of the purest souls I know. That's right, is it not? You require hosts with darkness. Murderers and thieves. Drug dealers and human traffickers. And there's a lot of you stuffed in there right now, isn't there? Too much for even the likes of Carl Taylor. Maybe Bateman would have been the right fit, but James... No, no. James was a beautiful human being and I'll destroy you for taking him from me."

He laughed... and laughed... and laughed...

The sound boomed off the walls. He wasn't supposed to be laughing.

"Do you think me an idiot?" he snapped. "I know this form cannot hold me. I merely needed a quick getaway and a lure for you." His lips curled into a twisted smile.

He looked around at the Warriors on the floor. "For all of you…you've become quite a nuisance and I thought it'd be a grand opportunity to take a chunk out of your forces." He whistled, and all the many faces of gymgoers I had seen over the years slowly walked in through the open gym door. There had to be more than thirty of them. He'd possessed them all. All of these people. All these humans who now had to die.

My heart stopped.

Among them, was Tony Marques.

"Tony," I breathed. He made his way from the group and took a place next to Erebus.

"Oh. Do you like this one?"

The Warriors, sensing the impending battle, stood to their feet and closed ranks around my back. One of Erebus's troops pulled the shutter down, trapping us inside.

"Do you understand how long I've waited for this?" James's mouth was practically frothing. Blood started to drip from his lips as the force of Erebus and his rage overwhelmed James' pure body. My eyes stung and panic started taking over me.

This had never been about James for him. He had used him as a ploy to get me here. To wipe out the key players in the Sina family. To eliminate the prophesied Warrior who it was foreseen would end him. Nicholas had been right to try and keep me away.

I thought of the efforts I had taken to be here. Looking at James, I could see that he was gone, because surely... surely if he was still in there, he would be fighting. He would have pulled a miracle and shown them all, that humans were capable of being saved from these possessions.

The dagger shook in my sweaty hand. It was an ambush, more elaborate than their attempt at the station. I didn't know what to do. I just knew that I had to try something, or we would all be slaughtered. I gripped the hilt as tightly as I could and tried to steady my breathing. He started to speak again, turning his back on me as he prowled.

"Billions of years have passed since I last came face to face with Gaia and Selene. The two women who had become one in their efforts to vanquish me. All they did was delay the inevitable. Chaos will always win." I took my chance and jumped for him; the blade raised high in the air.

I got no further than that. I had forgotten that Erebus was one entity in many different places. He had seen me coming through the eyes of those who surrounded me, as they too, were him. What an idiot move!

I paid for it. He backhanded me, mid-flight, hurling me across the gym. I landed painfully in a pile of barbells.

That one move was all the Sina's needed to trigger their attack. The Warriors turned on the small, but powerful, Erebus army. I lifted my head from my crumpled position and saw the battle reign. Lois fought two men at once, two large balding men. She sliced one across the face, booted the other in the chest, then turned her blade on the first guy she'd slashed and rammed it into his side. Debbie and Nicholas were up against five of them. I said a silent prayer as I stopped being able to tell the difference between whose limb was whose.

I vomited again as I saw Marcus holding his own, the giant super soldier he was. He had made his way through a dozen or more, the bodies were piling, but then they'd realised who they needed to take down first. I saw Tony Marques make a beeline for Marcus. I couldn't watch. I tried to make out James amongst the madness, just as I had at the Police station. I'd lost him *again*. I cursed under my breath. Useless!

I jumped up and made my way through the fighting, towards Tony. One job at a time, I told myself. Tony saw me. Not Tony. Erebus. It was getting confusing and harder to compartmentalise. I ran at him. He didn't run away or run to me, like I thought he would. He did exactly as James had done on the Police station roof. His fist crashed into the floor and the whole building shook.

Several metal beams tumbled from the ceiling, taking out several of his own as well as Sarah.

Debbie saw and tried to make her way to her daughter. Tony didn't give them chance and punched the floor again, sending down more debris. My eyes started to flood. I backed into a corner and slid to the floor. What had I done?

I watched as Marcus realised what was happening. He finished off the three men who had been trying to take him down with dumbbells, and ran over to Sarah, to his granddaughter. He lifted a large metal beam off her middle, freeing two other Erebus at the same time. That's when it happened.

One of the Erebus, a large man with a tattoo on his neck, picked up a thin bar. In one fatal blow, he impaled Marcus, thrusting the bar through his stomach and straight out his back. I heard several cries from around the room. I couldn't make out who or where in particular they came from. Debbie fell to her knees before her father as Nicholas fought to keep the Erebus surrounding them at bay.

What have you done? My brain kept asking me the same question.

What have you done, what have you done, what have you done?

I was overwhelmed and useless and had been cocky and reckless. I'd had no plan running in here. How could I ever lead these people? They'd gotten it wrong. They'd all gotten it wrong. It couldn't have been me they were waiting for. I knew it couldn't have been. There'd been a terrible mistake and now they were all going to die for it. Marcus was on his knees, the bar had been pulled from him by the same Erebus and I could see him winding back, ready to go in for the kill. Everything seemed to move in a strange light.

Several Erebus had Lois pinned to the ground. Sheridan was being choked against a wall. Clint was trying to fend off the largest man in the room. Fredrick had been trying to get on top of Tony, and Ainsley had gone in for the final strike, his Stiléto at the ready.

I took a deep breath, ready to watch yet another person I loved perish... It didn't happen. Tony had used the unseen force of Erebus, and the two men flew against the wall with a crack. I saw James in the corner of my eye.

He was perched on top of a weights machine, watching his beautiful chaos scatter across the room. A look of pride and accomplishment on his face. *James.*

I thought back over everything he had ever done for me. I thought back to the fourteen-year-old girl on the mats. To the punches and the kicks. To the times I had cried after heartbreaks. I remembered all those fine moments we'd shared. Studying to be police officers, the beach, the fire, the love.

"Stop them!" Selene screamed in my mind.

I released the tension I hadn't realised I'd been holding in and lifted my hands in the air, ready to release my guilt. I let it out.

"Stop!" I cried.

My voice was louder than I had ever heard it. It pierced the eardrums of everybody in the room. Everyone stopped to hold their ears. I stood before them all, hoping the madness would end there. I looked up at James on his perch.

"Stop this," I demanded. "If you want me, you can have me. Let them go." James shook his head.

"But I already have you. And them. Why would I stop when I have you right where I want you?"

There was a sudden explosion and we all flew metres apart.

When I opened my eyes, the room was filled with smoke. But I remembered my training. I let my instinct guide me and my vision changed so I could make out what was going on.

The explosion had been the sound of the shutter door being blown off. The smoke was coming from a small smoke grenade. This, I remembered well. My heart sang as I realised what Marcus had been anxiously looking to the road for.

The reinforcements.

The Sina family had touched down in full. The Erebus were now massively outnumbered. Every face I had seen at the dining table, what seemed like another life ago, now swarmed the room. There was no hesitation, no conversation, no opportunity for the Erebus to take the upper hand.

"How cute you all look," I heard Nicholas sneer at them all as they were slaughtered.

My moment had arrived. James jumped down from his perch and I figured he'd decided to kill me after all. A few people tried to step in his way but were thrown aside like ragdolls for their efforts.

No.

His eyes were for me only. It didn't feel as thrilling as it should have. He reached me in seconds, and I tried to deflect but had lashed out awkwardly in panic. He wrapped his hand around my throat and in one smooth movement, lifted me into the air. I tried to gasp and gulp and beat him off. I could feel his flaking skin on my neck.

"James," I garbled out. A useless attempt to get through to him. He was gone. I repeated it on a loop in my head. *He is gone.*

As the blood started gathering in my head, threatening to explode my skull, it sank in. I'd fought James before. I wondered if his muscle memory was still there. If he was using James's techniques.

I grabbed hold of his arm and swung my legs up, wrapping them around his neck and twisting the weight of my body, to break his arm.

Snap.

Erebus screamed out. *Erebus. Erebus!* This was Erebus. Not James. James was gone. *This is a parasite.* I kept saying it in my head as I landed on the floor and didn't wait a second more before spinning and kicking up into his face. I let my Warrior instincts rule my body. The force of that one kick broke his jaw and I saw blood fly from his mouth.

I kicked again, sending his body shooting across the gym and landing with a *crack* as the concrete floor crunched under the impact. I looked up, allowing myself a brief glance at Marcus. The battle over around me. I could see the high number of Warriors had thinned the Erebus crowd. Debbie, Nicholas, Sheridan, Sarah and Lois were all knelt around Marcus. His large frame seemed so small as they gathered with him. I could tell they were saying goodbye. His wound was too great for him.

I gritted my teeth. The rage was there again. My hands lit and I felt the power raging through my veins. I turned to the body of James. Erebus had stood up and was watching me with a wicked smile across his lips. He nodded.

"That's right. Use what is mine to destroy me. Let the rage fill you. Look around. Look at the chaos I have brought upon you all. Look at the death and the destruction. You want the revenge and it should be yours."

Something clicked… He wanted this. This had been his game. To get me angry. To get me to use the powers we somehow shared.

But why? To what end? I thought, the wheels and cogs in my head turning. I couldn't do this. Not like this.

"I'm not like you," I said, barely above a whisper, but I knew by the drop in his smirk that he could hear me. "I'm not Erebus. I'm not part of you." I let go of the rage and allowed the fire to drip away into nothing. I bent down to the floor and picked up a discarded Stiléto. This felt right. "I'm a Warrior."

He started to run for me, and I remembered my training with Marcus. I'd remembered the whole thing. Every punch, every kick, every pain, broken bone, stab, scratch and praise.

I remembered every divine move.

I threw the blade at human speed and ran towards the flying dagger. James dodged it in the same smug way. I carried on running past him, at Warrior speed, I grabbed the hilt in the air and fell down, as I could feel the oily slick of Erebus energy rush up behind me.

I plunged the dagger backwards and this time I didn't stop. I pushed it as far in as I could, feeling the blood on my fist, the gristle of his sternum. I didn't turn. I didn't want to see. The job was nearly done, I could feel it, centimetres from his heart.

Just one more thrust. Then the impossible happened.

"Loz."

My world stopped.

Chapter Eighteen

I could feel his breath on my neck. His hair tickling my ear. The sweat on his brow, wetting my cheek.

"Loz?"

I slackened my grip, ever so slightly. It was another trick. It had to be another trick. I turned slowly. James fell forward and landed on top of me.

Our faces were so close. I put my hand on his shoulder and pushed him up so the blade wouldn't push in further under his own body weight.

"Loz," he whispered again. I could barely hear him. I looked up into his eyes. Those beautiful brown eyes. Golden in the sun. Bottomless in the moonlight. It was James. I knew it with every atom of my being. A strange whimper escaped my lips. The room had disappeared and there was only him.

I was ready. I was ready to let him go. Ready to believe he was dead the moment Erebus had taken possession of him. Ready to kill the Erebus that ravaged his body, along with the body of the man I loved.

And oh, God, did I love him.

But now? This changed everything. He wasn't dead. He was here. In front of me, inches away from my lips. The Stiléto still imbedded in his sternum.

"Hi," he laughed, weakly, as one breath.

"Hi."

Tears were streaming from my eyes. I didn't try to hold them in. He tried to say something else, but his breaths were uneven and strained.

"Don't try to speak," I whispered softly. He was dripping in sweat. I started to pull the blade back out and he groaned.

"No!" It was the loudest he'd spoken. I stopped.

"No?" I asked, trying not to shake.

"No." He whispered. "I can feel him still. Erebus. He's still there. You have to finish it. Keep going." I shook my head.

"I can't. You're there. You're in there. I can't." I could barely speak. I could barely breathe. My mind was scattered. He smiled at me in pain.

"You can." A tear formed in the corner of his eye and dropped on my face. "I was in agony. He was carving himself into my soul. I could read his thoughts. He wants an eternal darkness. Never ending. He'll kill you, Loz." He moaned again and gasped. I could feel his blood leaking around the blade. "I can't let him hurt you. Just… just do it. Just a little further. Let me go."

"No." I sobbed violently. "I love you," I cried. "I love you! I love you! I love you!"

He closed his eyes and smiled. A real smile. The smile I had seen every day since the first day I'd known him. The smile he gave me when I told a rude joke or beat him in boxing. The smile I lived for. He nodded his head.

"I love you more." He laughed and winced at the same time. "Always did. I was going to marry you one day."

I sobbed again. "Then marry me. Marry me, James. *Please.*" His smile faltered and a trickle of blood rolled down his chin. His energy was failing. He shook his head slowly.

"Don't think we've got time, Loz." I could feel him trying to push himself down onto the blade.

"Stop!" I screamed. "Stop!" He stopped and his next breath sounded like it had glass in his lungs.

"Kiss me," he said. It was a command, though I could barely hear him.

"Live," I begged. He was tired of my arguing, just like he always was. He grabbed my hand and moved it from his shoulder, resting it on the side of his face. I stroked his cheek and wiped away another one of his betraying tears. He let himself fall on top of the blade, his lips falling on mine. I kissed him, deeply. A kiss we had been saving for a moment far less tragic than this one. He found the strength to kiss me back, just for a moment. A wonderful, sweet embrace. I could feel his lips turn up into a smile and I twisted the knife into his heart, crying out as I felt his body fall limp. I held his head onto mine and kissed his cheek. I lay sideways so his body slipped from mine and, sitting up, I pulled him onto my legs, cradling as much of him as I could gather in my arms. I could see the black oil of Erebus's decaying body starting to pour from his nose, his mouth, his ears, his eyes. I wiped them away with the back of my hand, not wanting that *thing* to mar his beautiful face.

I looked down on him and felt the eyes of the room on me. My world had ended. My heart was broken. I could feel everything building within me. There was a tickle in the back of my mind, and I could sense Selene trying to reach out to me. Trying to comfort me from within.

I didn't want her. I didn't want any of this. I pushed back and sobbed over James's body. My hand held over the bloodied hole I had created, not wanting to look at it. It was too much. Everything was too much. The death that surrounded me was more than one person could bare. I wanted to scream. I wanted to burn the world down around us, because it just wasn't fair. I let it consume me. The grief. The feeling of loss, like my heart had been torn from my chest. I wished to be numb. I wished for my life to end. I wished for something beyond this world where I could meet with him again. Because, surely this wasn't happening. It couldn't be happening. How could anybody survive this? I wasn't strong enough. The ramblings of a mad woman consumed me. I heard sobbing behind me and dared a peek at the further destruction I had wrought.

Marcus lay, motionless and sickly pale, in the arms of his daughter. He was gone too. My throat burned. My heart ached.

I could feel the tickling again. I didn't want her. I just wanted James. I just wanted to not be alone. I tried to push her away, but she kept coming back. Exhausted, my defences fell away and I heard five words come through, clear as a bell.

The sacrifice has been made.

It came out of me, spilling over, rampant and ugly and loud. I let it out. I screamed and screamed and screamed. I felt everyone in the room drop to their knees. My voice reaching a pitch not of this Earth and I felt all the pain and all the betrayal burst out of me. It was exhausting and I could feel blood start to pour from my nose. I screamed again. My insides felt like they were about to tear me open from the sheer force as though something was trying to claw out of my body.

And suddenly. So suddenly that I would never be able to accurately replay the moment in my head… I felt… wonderful.

I felt relief and a surge of light, incredible, power course through me from depths I wasn't even aware I had. Goodness and kindness and miracles. I felt it all.

Then I saw it. Visible light filled the room. It burst from me, like rays from the sun. I let it take over and I could feel life. The breath of it, the beat of it, the intricate, delicate, twisting and turning of life force, brimming from me. I felt a thud under my hand. And then another one. And another one. And another one.

I blinked until the light had faded and I could see the room again. I looked down at my hand. The black oil had disappeared from his face. It was James's face. His skin didn't look mottled anymore. It was smooth and clean.

I realised the thud had come from him. His heartbeat. I moved my hand. The wound was gone. There was no evidence at all that it had ever been there, save for the hole in his shirt.

"James?" I whispered, barely a breath, not daring to believe it. "James?" I said a little louder.

There was a silence and then suddenly his lungs expanded. His mouth opened, gasping for breath, his eyes open wide.

"James!"

His eyes scanned the room and he whimpered as his gaze fell on mine. He was beyond surprised to see me and his hand went to his chest, where the dagger had gone in. Tears streamed down my face.

"James." His name felt like a wish in my mouth. He shook slightly as he lifted his hand and wiped my cheek.

"You're so beautiful." His eyes brimmed and I laughed.

"I can't believe it," I whispered. I twisted at his hair with my fingers and brushed the side of his cheek and traced his lips. I wanted to drink him in.

He looked at me like a Goddess, in awe of my presence. He was, I think, grateful to me. I was grateful to him. Grateful for all he was. His hand took mine and he kissed my palm several times before placing it on his heart.

"You're incredible, do you know that?" He spoke so only I could hear him. A laugh bubbled from my lips.

"I've heard some people say that." He laughed and I melted.

There were reverent tones of chatter around the room. A heavy, thick atmosphere of wonder hung in the air. The smog from the grenades and the explosion of the shutter door had almost entirely cleared.

James slowly pulled himself up to a sitting position and leaned into my shoulder for support. A large hand extended to him and we turned to look up at the offering. My breath caught in my throat.

Marcus.

He was alive. No trace of the pole that had impaled him. He strolled, comfortably, and heaved James to his feet. In the same motion, he wrapped James up into an embrace, patting him violently on the back, before grabbing me by the shirt and pulling me in too. The smell of sweat, aftershave and blood overwhelmed my nose and I dug my face in deeper, because I didn't want either of them to disappear.

"I can remember so many things."

Everybody turned to face Tony Marques. He looked around at his gym, as though he didn't realise it was entirely demolished. "A world I've never known." He wiped a streak of black tar-like substance from under his nose. There was a shift around the room, and the bodies of the people who had laid dead on the floor, began to rise, all wiping the same black proof of Erebus's demise, from their noses. The Warriors converged and held their Stilétos high, prepared to fight again.

"Wait!" I commanded. They looked like they didn't want to wait, but still respected me enough to lower their weapons. I slowly made my way to Tony. He seemed in distress. I held up my hands to show I meant no harm. "It's okay. You're okay." He shook his head.

"How can I… I know so much?" He held his head. I rested my hands on his face and he looked at me with awe. "Theia," he breathed. I shook my head.

"It's Lauren, Tony. You remember me?" He nodded his head. "Of course, I remember you, Lauren. You're - You're something different. The girl with the false name." I looked deep into his eyes. The feeling of sickly oil on my skin was gone. Erebus was gone. The dead had risen, and they were free from Erebus's influence. But there was something else. I couldn't quite put my finger on it. I turned to the Sinas.

"Listen to me. They're not Erebus anymore. Pay attention to your instincts. You've taught me a lot these past few days. More than I ever thought possible. The one thing you've all said, the only constant... was to trust my instincts. Well, my instincts have saved my life, so many times already. Trust your instincts now. What do they tell you?"

I was met with silence as they side eyed one another. Sheridan stepped forwards and looked into a large bald man's face. He took a moment as he considered.

"They're... They're healed." He touched the man's chest. "I put my blade right here."

"Not just healed," Debbie corrected. "Resurrected."

"And exorcised of their possessing entity," Sarah added. Marcus moved around the room, taking in the people. They all looked like they needed a stiff drink.

"There's more," he murmured, running his hand through his hair as he tried to pinpoint what it was. "There's more." He stopped in front of Tony. "I can feel it."

Tony smiled. "I can feel it too, mate."

I looked around. I could feel something, but I wasn't sure what it was. I looked at James, who, to be frank, looked better than I'd ever seen him. He glowed in a very specific and very familiar way. My heart fluttered with excitement.

"It can't be," I sighed. I paced over to him, slowly, stopping centimetres away from his face. His eyes hooded, and definitely fighting the urge to kiss me. My body yearned for him, but now wasn't the time. Something beyond what I had learnt in my short time as a member of this world. Something I believed would change things for these people, forever. Perhaps for me too. I spoke in hushed tones.

"*Lead the Universe into a new age*," I quoted. I lifted my hands and stroked his face, lowering them to his chest. I could feel it radiating off of him. Something incredible and I suddenly felt closer to this man than I had felt in my entire life. I felt I had been given a gift that nobody could ever take from me again. I would never feel alone ever again. I looked into his eyes. "You're like me."

He nodded.

"I can feel it. Like my skin is a light and it feels…"

"Alien? Infuriating?" I offered. He laughed his warm, sexy laugh and I had to take a step back when he said, "Incredible."

I turned and faced the room, preparing myself to change their lives forever. I had done something I didn't even know was possible. Something exhausting and powerful and beautiful and incomprehensible and beyond all… impossible.

"They're all Warriors now."

The room erupted.

I wiped the blood from under my nose and looked down at it on the back of my hand. A million thoughts danced around my head as I released that wave of… I don't even know what. That feeling of euphoria that erupted from within me – and nearly killed me – had brought James back from the dead. It had brought everybody back from the dead… but it hadn't brought them back as humans. They had been resurrected as Warriors.

The Sina family started questioning the newly born Warriors, touching them, reaching out for the same familiarity I had felt. Marcus came over, Debbie and Nicholas by his side.

"You brought me back from the dead, my girl." He laughed. "Not really sure what we do now." He looked around at the room full of people.

"We should send a message to Celest," Debbie advised. "She needs to know about this."

"Agreed."

"I think we should take them with us. They're going to be confused and they'll need guidance," Nicholas suggested. I giggled.

"Glad I came?" I asked him. He rolled his eyes and Debbie elbowed him. He laughed.

"Actually, yes I am," he confessed. Then, "I'm sorry."

I waved him off. "Nice to know you care." He winked in a very, *I've got you* kind of way.

James had been standing as close to me as he could, and I slipped my hand down to intertwine my fingers with his.

"I need to make a few calls. See if we can get a few cars down here before the authorities show up." Marcus pulled out a mobile phone and tutted as he realised his phone screen was cracked. I'm not sure what he expected.

He walked away, dialling carefully around the shards. Debbie turned to me and James. "What will you do now? This is all a little...unprecedented. I'm not sure what we thought would happen, but… it wasn't this. I imagine there'll be questions. What comes next and all that."

I nodded. "I think I have a lot of questions, myself." I peeked up at James to see what he wanted to do.

"I'll follow you wherever you go." My heart sang.

I turned to Debbie. "This isn't our life anymore. I can't see how we could ever return to what we used to be. I guess… I welcome what is meant for me. In your world. Erm…could we stay with you?"

Debbie laughed. "Of course. We'd be honoured."

Nicholas patted James on the shoulder.

"It'd probably be safest anyway. Remember, Erebus is spread thin, but he is still connected on a higher level to every part of himself, right across the globe. He'll know what happened here tonight. He won't let this lie.

Lauren… he'll come for you. You can bet on it." I shrugged and looked up at James.

"Just let him try."

Chapter Nineteen

By the time it had been arranged to have the formerly Erebus-possessed, formerly dead, currently resurrected, newly-made Warriors taken somewhere safe, the sun had cleared the horizon and was warming the day up in typical heatwave style.

Marcus had gone in the large convoy with the majority to be checked over, along with everybody else who had died, to make sure they were in perfect health. James had been asked to go with them as well, but as I had expected, he'd point blank refused. I didn't think he'd be leaving my side for quite some time, and to be honest, I would have super glued our hands together if I'd had the paste to do it.

I hugged Marcus goodbye before he left and he nearly crushed James when it was time for them to part ways. I recalled his story of James's mother and their involvement in the story of her death. I remembered the way he had acted when James had been taken by Erebus, like he was mourning him along with poor Lewis. I could tell now that he really did care for the baby he'd saved and returned to his father. I thought about that a little more. The coincidence of it all. I wasn't sure that I still believed in coincidences.

We stood outside, watching the sun rise above the trees and the convoys turning the corner onto the main road in the distance. The gym had been all but destroyed and I wondered whether Tony would care too much in the grand scheme of things. I planned on asking Debbie where everyone had been taken so I could write or maybe visit as soon as was possible. We needed to have a long conversation, I thought. The whole thing must have felt like they were being sequestered away by the secret service for experimentation. Though, they shared the same memories as the born Warriors now, so I supposed they would find a calm trust in that.

James seemed different, which was perfectly understandable. His eyes seemed to hold the weight of a thousand years. I leant my head on his shoulder.

"We'll need to find a new boxing ring," I jested. He chuckled and I felt him rumble as his shoulders lifted up and down.

"I'm sure we'll find a place."

Nicholas whistled. "Alright children, cars ready. Let's go." Debbie pulled up in front of us, and Nicholas opened the back doors.

"I call shotgun," he said.

We took a detour to James's flat and then to mine to gather some essentials. It didn't look like we'd be returning home for a while. Where was home anyway? Maybe I didn't need a home. It certainly didn't feel like anywhere near here, anymore. It's strange how much can change in just a few days. Really, everything had changed in that one night... in that one moment.

A part of me was grateful to Debbie. In her mind, she was completing a task she had been created to complete. One more mission. One more death. To me, it was the opening of a door into the life I was meant for. I'd spent my whole childhood out of sync with everyone and everything. Bouncing from school to school and family to family isn't fun for a child. The only time I'd ever felt grounded was with James and his father. Now, even that had changed a little. James would have to leave his father for quite some time, according to Nicholas. Just while the dust settles. We may even have to have him moved to a safe house. Nothing was certain yet.

We climbed into the back seat of the car. I wriggled over because I didn't want James to do anything strenuous. He told me I was being ridiculous because, when I'd brought him and everyone else back, they had been completely healed of their afflictions. I however, despite my fast Warrior healing, was still recovering from the night's ordeals. Wielding that much power had certainly taken a toll on my body and I welcomed food and a warm bed... Preferably with James lying next to me...

Naked...

I shook off the need for him and turned my attention out of the window as we set off towards the main road. It seemed as though everything was brighter and more vivid now. The past few days had put everything in a shadow and I never really trusted what I was seeing. I never trusted myself. I thought Selene and Gaia were ruining my life. I felt like a brat, looking back. I understood in that moment that not everything can be constantly perfect. You have to take the good with the bad. If the 'bad' meant that I had to leave my life behind and train and study and prepare to take on a beyond powerful entity to save the universe… well then, so be it. Because, the 'good' gave me the power to bring the people I loved back from the dead. It gave me the power to free humans from the possession of Erebus without having to kill them. Even Gaia wasn't known to have been able to do that. This was something new. Something unique.

A fox ran by the side of the road, and I watched as it dove into a deep green bush. I smiled to myself. I felt so safe, which I knew was stupid because this war was far from over. But right in that moment, I felt safe.

We arrived at James's place. He lived on the fourth floor in a one bedroom. If I was ever over at his place and we'd had a little too much to drink, I'd take his bed and he'd always take the couch. He was always the gentleman… unless we were in the ring. That was a different story. We all headed up together – safety in numbers – but I had hoped we would be alone. I didn't want to hold his dying words over him, but I was a little (a lot) curious as to how much of that had been because he was afraid and how much had been the truth about how he felt for me. He'd said he was going to marry me one day. That had been his presumption, or so he said. In any other scenario I would have taken that to be him giving off some pretty strong signals. I, however, basically told him the truth in a moment I couldn't put down to being close to certain death.

The situation had been dire, I'll admit. He'd been pretty cosy with me on the ride to his place, but we tended to be that way anyway. That came from the kind of bond we had. We were extremely comfortable in each other's presence.

I took a sneaky look up at him as we climbed the stairwell. He seemed to be in his own head. Again, perfectly understandable. I couldn't imagine what he was thinking. Here I was, contemplating whether he saw me as more than a friend, and he was likely mapping out the rest of his existence as a Warrior. I'd adapted quite well to the idea, probably because I never really knew where I came from and it was a novelty to discover something about my heritage. For James, this was completely alien. He thought he knew who he was. The situations were very different. My Warrior blood came from my ancestors, his came from… well… me. Yeah. It was totally different.

We came to his door, number one hundred and eleven. He turned to Nicholas and Debbie. "It's a bit of a mess. You can wait out here if you want."

"Not likely," snorted Nicholas. James shrugged his shoulders and let us all in. His place was actually immaculate, as always. Nicholas clicked his tongue.

"If this is a mess, what does clean look like?" He flounced himself onto the couch and pulled Debbie with him, tickling her. She elbowed him to release herself. It was sweet. To be like teenagers in love after centuries together. I met James's eye and smiled sheepishly. He cocked his head towards his bedroom.

"Come help me pack." I followed him.

James has always been quite simple and unmaterialistic. We had his bag packed in less than twenty minutes. Just the essentials, as instructed. Clothes, toothbrush, cash. He wasn't ever one for keepsakes and all the trinkets around the room, he declined when I advised he should pack them. However, when I picked up a picture of us and Sensei Clarke in the Dojo, he took it without a word and placed it in his bag. We'd been kids in that photo. I had been sixteen and James Eighteen. We had been awarded first and second place medals in a Judo competition and were smiling like we'd just won gold in the Olympics. It had been a simpler time… though it wasn't hard to be. He zipped up the front compartment and slapped his knees.

"That should do it." I picked up a teddy bear I'd won at a charity's fate and put it in front of my face, making its head tilt animatedly.

"You don't want to take Mr. Snuggles?" He laughed.

"Nah, I think he can stay and guard the flat." I nodded and chucked the bear onto his bed. I looked at it and then at James. I thought I could see a glint in his eye that told me his mind was teetering around the same point. He cleared his throat and a rare shyness came over him.

"Erm – yeah. Some things were said." I bit my lip.

"Some things were said, indeed." He ran a hand through his hair.

"I just wanted you to know –" The door to his room opened and Nicholas stepped in.

"We need to get moving. Are you all packed?" I swore in my head. Just a few more seconds and I would have had my answer. James looked a little irritated too and I didn't know if that boded well or not.

"Yeah, good to go."

My place was the next stop. I really didn't have many keepsakes either, but I did have a few cute outfits that I wouldn't have left behind if you'd paid me. And nobody was paying me, so I definitely needed to grab the cash savings I had stashed underneath my mattress.

The ride over was quiet. Nicholas had definitely cottoned on to the fact he'd interrupted a vital conversation and turned the radio up to cover the awkwardness. I didn't like it. It was the kind of thing I was afraid of. The reason I hadn't told him about my feelings before.

"I'm not sure I like this album," he said, referring to the singer on the radio. "Her last two were so much better, don't you agree?"

James smiled, politely.

"Yeah," Nicholas continued. "Her first album was definitely the best. Her career kind of took off from the second album though. This one is just okay."

James held my hand the whole time.

When we arrived, James and I jumped out of the car first and put our hands on the front two doors so that Debbie and Nicholas stayed put.

"Why don't you guys keep watch from out here?" I suggested with as light a tone as I could manage. Nicholas pushed his door and James promptly closed it again. Debbie cottoned on as fast as I'd imagined she would. We really just wanted five minutes to talk. Debbie rested her hand on Nicholas's shoulder and they silently let us go. She winked at me to signal that she understood. Good looking out, Debs.

I walked into my flat first. It felt alien. The last time I'd been here was the morning I'd woken up after my rendezvous with Debbie and the start of all of this. I stepped over the threshold a completely different person. Had it really only been three days? Or was it four? I'd completely lost track.

I walked straight to the bathroom and picked up my toothbrush, toothpaste and a couple of travel sized shampoos and conditioners. They were leftovers from the last time James and I had had a training night in London and had been put up in a semi-decent hotel. We had played Russian roulette with our bank cards at dinner. He copped for the bill.

I walked into my bedroom and pulled my suitcase down from the top of my wardrobe. It was only a small one, the kind you take on the plane with you for overhead baggage. I had started throwing in my favourite summer dresses when I realised James wasn't with me.

"James?" I called. He didn't answer, so I walked back out into the living room. He stood, staring out of the window.

I'd been blessed with quite a nice view. There was a park over the way, and a lake with ducks and swans nipping at passers-by who they thought may have bread. There were sections of open land and in one spot we could see a dog walker throwing a ball for his beloved companion. The Labrador bounded over to catch the tennis ball, its long fluffy tail, swishing with happiness as it caught it mid-air and brought it back to its best friend, covered in saliva. I smiled, then turned to James.

"You okay?" I asked, gently.

He nodded, but then dragged his hands down his face in a way which suggested he wasn't all that okay after all. He laughed into his hands and then dropped them to look at me. His cheeks were flushed.

"You don't seem okay."

He laughed again and shook his head. I realised he wanted to say something but didn't know how to say it. I helped him along towards the direction I assumed he was going.

"Look," I started. "It's okay, James. It was in the moment. There was a lot going on. I understand. I... I honestly..." My stomach twisted with nerves. "I'm going to say it again, because I've wanted to say it since the day I met you and so much has happened that I hope it doesn't ruin what we have if I do say it, because I do and it's the truth and if I were you, I'd want to know, but if I'm wrong to say it, then please, just... don't get all weirded out and ignore me or think you have to stay away because you know I can handle it and it changes nothing —" I was rambling and I knew it. I nearly threw up as I said the next words. "James, I love you and not in the way a friend loves a friend and definitely not in the way a sister loves her brother. I love you. Head over heels, want to hire a skywriter to put it in the clouds for you, want to cut my heart out, love you. Completely and utterly. There." I was breathless and had said the whole thing to the floor. I turned and walked back into my bedroom to finish packing.

I probably should have stayed there instead of leaving the poor man alone with my confession, but I thought I knew what his reply would be and I thought it best if he just texted it to me from the living room while I buried my head in my suitcase.

I heard my door squeak open. I turned to tell him that he really didn't have to worry about anything - but I never got the chance.

He kissed me.

He really kissed me, smothering anything I might have said with his lips.

One of his hands reached behind my head and the other grabbed my waist. He pulled my body close to his and our lips pushed together. I'd never felt anything like it before. There was a connection I couldn't explain. Every molecule of my body wanted his.

I leaned into him, trying to fill the tiniest spaces that separated him from me. Our lips moved in a synchronised rhythm and everything just felt right. I ran my hands through his hair and when he moaned, I pulled us both onto the bed.

There was an animalistic instinct to the way we moved with each other and a part of me was reminded of how we fought in the ring. But this was, of course, better than that. For a start, nobody was getting a bust lip.

Hmm, there was an idea.

I bit down on his lip and he kissed me harder. He felt it too. A hunger that only the other one of us could fill. My skin felt like it was on fire and there was a burning in the pit of my stomach. He pulled at my shirt and lifted it over my head, running his hands through my hair kissing my neck. I'd just started to tug at his clothes when – for the love of all that is holy – a car horn blared from the car park outside. James moaned, and not in a good way. He stopped what he'd been doing, which was really annoying because he was doing it very well, and rested his forehead on mine. Our breathing was erratic from the workout we'd barely begun. The car horn continued.

"I'm going to kill him," James grunted, his voice like gravel.

"Don't stop," I whispered to him. He laughed and started kissing me again. The horn beeped four times in rapid succession, then again for a drawn-out period. I laughed into James's mouth and he laughed back.

"What are the chances we'll get an opportunity to be alone like this again any time soon?" I shrugged my bare shoulders and pulled the strap of my bra back into its place.

"James, we're not even alone now." I giggled. I really didn't want this to end. James passed me the shirt that he'd thrown to the side, his body still hovering over mine. I pulled it over my head, and he helped me pull it down, taking his time, his fingers trailing across my skin. Trust him to make putting clothes *on* sexy.

"For the record," he said, leaning closer to my face. "I really do love you. And I truthfully, always did." He kissed me and I smiled. When he pulled away, I winked at him.

"Gonna marry me one day, yeah?" I said, poking him in the stomach. He laughed at that.

"Oh, something I said in my biggest moment of weakness, and you're going to hold it over me?" I nodded. "Fine," he said. "In for a penny, in for a pound… I am absolutely going to marry you one day." I smiled up at him.

"Always good to know where a man stands."

"I'm standing over you."

"Yes, you are." His lips parted and he leaned closer to me, that fire starting to burn again. Alas, nothing can be completely perfect and so Nicholas continued his assault of the car horn, preventing James from continuing his assault of me.

 He stood up off the bed, pulling me up with him and we made our way to the window.

It was evident. Nicholas was repetitively hammering the car horn and Debbie was smacking him repeatedly in the arm, begging him to stop.

 "It's a good job you're moving. He must really be annoying the neighbours."

 "Let's go," I said. I quickly grabbed the rest of my things and we headed back down to the car. Nicholas was tapping his watch dramatically as we walked out and Debbie shook her head.

Chapter Twenty

We arrived at the large Sina Manor at two in the afternoon and everybody was exhausted. The house was full. The Warriors who had joined the battle in the gym had returned to the manor to recuperate. The new Warriors and Marcus had been taken somewhere else, though nobody was entirely certain where at that moment. It was apparently another safe house, similar to Lesley and Christian's, but a lot bigger. That made sense, given the large number of people who needed to be catered for.

Someone was cooking and it smelled heavenly, giving me that comforting feeling of coming home. We opened the door to see Serenity and her cousins running by. They were very excited to see Debbie and Nicholas. Serenity threw herself around Nicholas's legs. He made a big show and dance of how heavy she was, while dragging his leg across the floor and calling her his *Little Monkey*. Debbie had one of the teenage members of the family take our bags upstairs for us, ignoring my protests that we could do it ourselves. I had hoped James and I might have been able to use getting settled in as an excuse for being alone for a bit. I'm not saying we'd have managed to finish what we'd started at my flat, what with a house absolutely brimming with people, but we could have had a pretty intense make out session.

When James headed into the kitchen to ask if anybody needed help, I pulled Debbie to one side.

"Could I ask you a quick question. It's a bit personal."

Debbie smiled knowingly and cocked her head towards a door on the left of the hallway. I followed her into a small sitting room. I was surprised any room in this house was small, but it was rather cosy. Maybe that had been the point. There were two armchairs, a coffee table and a fireplace. I wondered, idly, if Warriors had therapy. This would have been the perfect room for it.

Debbie sat on the side of one of the chairs and crossed her arms, tilting back slightly. She thought a moment.

"There is something I may have neglected to tell you. Mainly, because it didn't seem important at the time... but now, I suppose it's rather an important piece of information." I raised my eyebrows.

"Please don't leave me in suspense."

She nodded.

"Do you recall me explaining when and why our aging process started to slow down so much?"

I nodded. "Because the Warrior numbers were dwindling in relation to the growing power of Erebus." Debbie nodded.

"Exactly… so, I remember you were quite taken aback when Nicholas and I told you we had fourteen children."

"Yeah..." I said slowly. She seemed embarrassed and something started to click.

"Well… slowing down our body clocks isn't the only way nature has of increasing the Warrior population." My eyes widened.

"Are you telling me that there's a Warrior gene that makes Warriors… you know?"

"Hot for other Warriors like rabbits in Spring?" she suggested. My mouth dropped open. I grew a little worried for a very specific reason.

"But does that mean that James's feelings for me could just be because he's a Warrior now? Like, his genetic makeup is making him feel that way towards me?"

Debbie shook her head ferociously.

"Not at all. Our genes make that connection stronger. It doesn't create it. Take me and Nicholas, for example. We've been together for centuries. Neither has been unfaithful to the other. Those… feelings… they aren't for every Warrior. Lust and love are two different things. I love Nicholas. Everything else is just… heightened."

I nodded, a wave of relief washing over me.

"You guys need to be… erm… careful," she continued. "You should ignore, entirely, the things you think you know about female anatomy. It's all-round baby." She chuckled, clearly getting more uncomfortable by the second. The conversation really was starting to feel like a mother having *the talk* with her daughter. I laughed.

"Got it. Warriors are super fertile."

Debbie nodded. "Essentially."

There was a light knock on the door, and Debbie opened it. Serenity came in, her long hair draped over her shoulders.

"My darling!" Debbie swept her up in a big hug, the little girl's dress swayed around her ankles. She laughed and pushed away her mother's kisses.

"Mum! Stop!" I chuckled at how serious she was trying to be, this tiny little girl with the command of a Warrior in training.

"What can I do for you?" Debbie asked, setting her daughter back on the ground. Serenity turned to me.

"My Daddy said you need to come upstairs." I looked at Debbie, who just shrugged and turned back to Serenity.

"Did Daddy say what for?"

"The painting has changed."

Well, she wasn't kidding. The painting *had* changed. James had been called up as well, along with a few other, equally confused, family members. They ran their hands along the walls and took photographs. They asked questions. Bemused children sat crossed legged watching their parents, aunts, uncles, brothers and sisters lose their minds.

I seemed to be the only one who could make sense of it. We knew that Celeste and all the other soothsayers who came before her could see the future only to a certain point. The more powerful an Erebus chain of events became, the shorter the line of sight.

Except, that's what never really made much sense to me. Erebus couldn't penetrate the mind of Warriors. Celeste, the artist, was a Warrior. As far as we were aware, Erebus had strength as one being, beyond anything we could fathom, but as it stands, he was still in pieces across the globe. Sure, he was making a comeback, and he'd found a way to bring the larger pieces of himself together by way of certain water sources (another issue to look into, another time). I didn't see any way he, it, the thing, whatever you want to call it, could have had the ability to block the future… but… he could create a smoke screen. He, perhaps, had the strength to trick a soothsayer. Potentially, he could make them forget what they'd seen, in the same way Debbie had lost her memories when she faced Carl Taylor in his cell.

I ran my hands along the edges, where one of the children had discovered the paint peeled away to reveal another painting hidden behind. That's how this image had come to change. It had been there all along.

I wondered if higher powers were at play. Debbie explained that the paint had been derived from crushed moon rock, mixed with other substances, so that the room and the painting would be protected from anybody under the possession of Erebus, should they gain access to the house.

A part of me wondered if Selene had a hand in this. You see, the painting beneath the painting had prophesied James's death, prior to his resurrection. I believed Selene knew that if I'd seen the painting before everything hit the fan, I would have taken James and ran for the hills. I would have never helped them, never learned as much as I have, and I certainly wouldn't have been at that gym to sacrifice James and discover that I had the power to heal, resurrect the dead and, best of all, exorcize Erebus without having to kill the host.

Granted, this hadn't been a party trick, and the power it took had nearly melted my brain, but I was sure I'd be able to work on it and grow my strength, thus improving my powers and abilities. I hadn't even scratched the surface of what lay within me.

I had changed over thirty human's genetical makeup in one swoop and had literally birthed a new species of Warrior. These people, James included, were made from the bones of Eden *and* Gaia. I wondered how this would play out for them and was excited for what discoveries lay ahead for James.

He came beside me and held my hand as we both took in the tragic scene. I hadn't even realised that the white dress in the painting had been the nightie I wore that night. It made sense in hindsight, the tears that my image shed. We turned at the same time to the wall above the door. The area that had been entirely black before. It depicted a large mountain that nobody seemed to recognise except for Nicholas and Debbie. They'd been discussing in hushed tones when I approached them.

"Something to share with the group? Because I don't have a clue what that means." Debbie smiled and made eye contact with Nicholas. Nicholas nodded his head.

"No... I mean… yes, we know this mountain."

"Okay?" I waved my hand in a *Do Continue* gesture. Debbie sighed.

"That's where Celeste lives," she whispered, barely loud enough for me to hear and I was standing inches away from her. She looked around to make sure nobody was listening. "Her whereabouts has remained a secret for three centuries. Since the time she painted this room. My Mother swore to protect her. What you have to understand is that the living soothsayer is our only edge over Erebus. She knows things before they happen, she tells us when something big is coming, up to a certain point of course." I nodded and looked at the peeled off black paint around the floor. "If the painting has progressed, then…then she can finally see the next chapter, she can see the future beyond this."

"But this hasn't happened yet. Unless England has grown some wicked mountains since the last time I checked. So, is this the future?"

"I don't see any other explanation," she replied.

We stared at the painting for another hour or so before breaking for dinner. The family had assembled in the dining room again, but I felt it was a little too crowded and my tired eyes couldn't cope with the conversation of well over fifty people. The family split into groups, the largest taking the table, and the rest dispersing between sitting rooms and the patio out back.

I decided to join the people outside, because frankly, they were my favourites. Sheridan and Lois sat together with Sarah, eating a plate of fries that I thought needed a lot more ketchup. Clint was bouncing Serenity on his knee and singing a song about a horsey that *trots, canters and gallops*, which ended with her going into the ditch as he threw her across the patio. She rolled over, laughed and ran back to him, singing, "Again, again!" I shook my head and laughed. These kids were made of steel.

Debbie, Nicholas, James and I all sat on a large wooden swing, eating hot dogs. The setting was a lot less formal than the last time we'd eaten together and I felt comfortable in one of the summer dresses I'd packed from my flat. My bare feet scuffed on the floor as I rocked us backwards and forwards.

Debbie was pointing up at the darkening night sky and arguing that the star that had appeared first was Jupiter and not Venus. Nicholas slapped her hand down playfully.

"Debbie, I'm telling you, the brightest star in the sky is Venus. So, doesn't it just make logical sense for that star to be Venus."

She shook her head. "Okay, but Jupiter is actually the planet that's brightest in the sky! I read it somewhere. It's a common misconception that it's Venus."

"Where on Earth did you read *that?*"

"I can't remember!"

"Because it's not true. You just don't want to admit that you're wrong."

"Can someone just Google it *please!* And babes, when we find out you're wrong, you're giving me shoulder massages for a week."

"Go for it, Debs. Google away."

She sighed loudly. "My phone's in the house."

I looked up and saw that the star was moving. I burst out laughing. "Erm, guys. Hate to get involved in your lovers' spat, but that right there is a plane." They both leaped forwards and squinted. A brief silence fell as they monitored its movements.

"Suppose it doesn't really matter then," Nicholas muttered, leaning back on the swing. Debbie continued to watch, then leaned back and crossed her arms.

"I'm still right about the Jupiter thing."

Nicholas rolled his eyes and pinched her hot dog from her lap, biting into it. She snatched it back. I smiled at them both and leaned into James's shoulder.

Everything felt perfect. The night was warm and the stars (and the occasional plane) were starting to appear. We had good food and better company. I was in the arms of the man I loved. I knew that hard times lay ahead and that I should revel in the moments of peace and happiness whenever I found myself in them. This was one of those moments.

I wiped a smudge of mustard off the corner of James's mouth. He leaned down and kissed my cheek three times before placing a kiss on my mouth, lingering for a moment. I kissed him back. I reminded myself that I needed to speak with him about what Debbie had told me in the therapy looking room, about the *feelings* we had when we were close like that. I forced myself to pull away.

I could tell by the look in his eyes he could have carried on for an infinite amount of time, but if he did, it would have been awkward for the surrounding family. Serenity didn't need to see us making out on their garden swing.

I swallowed and murmured, "You good?"

He smiled. "Yeah, I'm good. You good?"

"Great." I nodded.

"Good."

"Good."

The swing shifted as somebody stood up. Debbie took a few steps forward, focusing her eyes on something in the distance. We all followed her gaze. When I realised who it was, making their way towards the house, I jumped up. Serenity had seen him too and she darted towards the visitor. As he came closer to the house, the little girl jumped on him and held his neck, hugging him tightly. He laughed and patted her back, coming to a halt just before us.

"Amos," I said, smiling at him. "Good to see you again."

He smiled widely.

"You were everything I expected you to be… or so I hear." I nodded. Word travelled fast amongst these people. My people. I felt warm again.

"What brings you here?" Debbie asked. "I can't remember the last time you left the dealership."

Amos shrugged. "It's been over a year since I last strayed more than three miles away, that's for sure. To see this little one on her birthday, if memory serves." He set Serenity down, then turned and eyed James.

"Let me see you!" His hands clapped the side of his legs. James looked at me for assurance. I winked at him and he stood up. Amos put his hands on the side of James's face and inhaled sharply.

"It's true then. I feel the bond of a fellow Warrior coursing through you." He kissed James on either cheek. James raised his eyebrows and laughed awkwardly.

"Welcome to the family, James."

James shook Amos's hand. "Thank you, Sir." Always the gentlemen. Amos stepped back and suddenly remembered why he'd taken his trip.

"That's not what I came for, actually." He patted his jacket, dipped his fingers into his top pocket and handed an envelope to Debbie. "A telegram arrived at the dealership this morning… I haven't opened it. It had your name on the envelope… but look at the postage stamp."

I leaned over Debbie's shoulder and saw a cluster of mountains. My eyes widened.

"The Himalayas," Debbie gasped, looking at Nicholas. Nicholas looked around at the group. She turned the envelope over, opened it, and pulled out a letter. It had six short lines, written in a delicate cursive handwriting.

My Dearest Debbie,

My sight has returned.

I must see her, and I must see him.

Bring them to me.

The future is short, and it is imminent.

All my love,
Celeste

I looked back at Debbie's face for clarification as to what exactly this meant. The atmosphere was electric. There was an element of fear and excitement in a bundled haze. What did this mean?

"Debbie?" I prompted. She turned to me and James.

"You should both go and pack. We'll leave first thing in the morning."

"I'll join you," Amos said. "You'll need me to get through the final days of the journey." Nicholas nodded shortly. Debbie turned and looked at Serenity, who had gone back to Clint for another bout of horsey rides. Nicholas gave her shoulder a squeeze.

"She'll be safe here. The time will fly, don't worry." Debbie reached for his hand and nodded. "She's strong," he whispered in her ear.

"What's happening?" I asked, confused.

"Celeste has requested your presence. We have to go to her as soon as we can. It's quite a journey to get there, so be prepared for a lot of leg work." I looked at James, who asked the question.

"Where is *there*?"

Debbie handed him the envelope and answered, "Nepal Himalayas."

My mouth dropped open.

"The mountain?" I breathed. James held my hand tight as he shared the anticipation. It seemed we wouldn't be granted any time to ourselves after all. I sighed.

"Alrighty then."

The night carried on in a warm summer's blur. I remained content in the moment, despite the uncertainty ahead. All that mattered, in that moment, was that James would be with me the whole way. I turned to him.

"You with me?"

He smiled and kissed my forehead.

"Where you lead, I will follow."

Acknowledgements

For the few people who took this journey with me,

My thanks go to my editor, Joshua Potts. Thank you for all your hard work, feedback and belief in me and my ideas. You're a true talent and a great friend.

I thank my family for listening to me ramble on at the most inopportune times, about my crazy ideas and for all the therapy you gave me in my moments of doubt.

I can't wait to hear what you think of this one. It's been an absolute blast to write.

The biggest thanks of all goes to you, the reader. Thank you for taking a chance on Selene. I hope you stick with Lauren on her journey to Nepal as the story continues in my next book in the series: 'Gaia.'

It's going to blow you away.

All my love,
Rebecca
x

Printed in Great Britain
by Amazon